2065

In The Beginning

2065

In The Beginning

Krista Markowitz

Mauka Press

Pacifica, California

2065

in The Beginning

Copyright © 2011 Krista G. Markowitz
Mauka Press
Pacifica, California
www.tipperwillow.com

ISBN 978-0-9833579-0-2

Photography and cover design:
Barbara With: www.barbarawith.com

Acknowledgments

For their delicious help in editing this book, multicolored bubbles of joy to Hal Markowitz, Michele Jarvis, and Ryckje Wagner. Whoop-whoop and warm thanks fly off to Barbara With for intuiting and creating the perfect cover.

And to those wily spirits who one breezy day last August showed me a vision of a future world and then said, "This is a book, Krista. Do you want to do it?" What can I say, guys? It's been a blast!

To Hal, Jenny, Wendy, and Tim
Family Extraordinaire!

~ Chapter 1 ~

September 22, 2064

    The ten-year-old boy looked up as he felt the whirring vibration deep in his chest. A ribbon of lavender light flowed through the sky high above him and disappeared. He felt the same flush of excitement whenever an air tram flew overhead. Three months before it had been an air tram or A.T. that carried Jeori*, traveling alone as was tradition, through the sky to his new home.

    During his first week of Past Class, Jeori had watched the vids of the way things were before the new tecks—those vehicles in all shapes and sizes speeding nose to tail over concrete tracts called "freeways." *Free* ways! What a stupid name! And there was nothing free about the people who traveled them either. They lived their lives hurrying back and forth to jobs they hated in crowded places called "cities" just so they could earn some stuff called "money." Jeori fingered the old coin his parents had given him—a "quarter" it was called. It hung from a chain around his neck. Dad had drilled it as a souvenir for Jeori right before he had left to come here. Yesterday he had painted it a shiny metallic blue.

    Jeori looked up again. He sensed another tram higher up and moving faster than the lavender line. It flashed into sight quickly, a streak of white that was here and gone again. The lowest tram, the slowest moving of the three, was not running today.

* "Jeori" is pronounced "Jori"

This was the powder blue line intended for tourists, and it only flew on weekends. Twice on Saturdays and Sundays it swooped low over hills and meadows, over villages and sea, and over the many quads and pods, the learning and living centers of Amerada.

Cleo was heading back to Art Pod when she came upon the new boy staring up at the sky. Was his name Jeori? *He must be part Native Ameradan with some—yes, Irish,* she thought as she quickly studied the boy's features; his brown skin and his bright blue eyes, the straight freckled nose and the high cheekbones. His dark hair highlighted with red was pulled back into a thick braid. It was a good look on him.

Jeori glanced over to see the older girl walking toward him. He couldn't remember her name, but he remembered her all right. Her spiked, white-blonde hair was hard to miss. And the fluid, confident way she moved made her stand out from everybody else, too. She reminded Jeori of one of those small, fast African cats.

The teenager raised her right hand and waved a quick hello as she passed. Then as she moved on, Cleo brought her hand down to her face to look at it again. She turned it slowly from side to side to catch the faint lines of light now patterned beneath the skin. She had waited so very long for this day, the day when she would finally have journey status, no longer just a child and student but a second level apprentice able to earn her own credits.

She could use those credits for the A.T. and for food and lodging while she was out exploring the world. Oh, the places she would visit!

Insertion of the network of tiny filaments hadn't hurt at all. She knew how to reach trance state. She'd known for years. She lay down on the cushioned table and traveled in her mind to her sanctuary, a garden she had first created with her imagination when she was four. She stayed there watching the leaves of her cherry tree swaying in the breeze, smelling the sweet roses, and listening to the bird songs until finally a voice called her out. And it was done!

At fourteen years of age, Cleo could now travel anywhere at all on the Earth—*when* she had enough credits. Every bit of work she did from here on would be recorded through the light webbing shining through the top of her hand.

The green light would flash briefly through her skin as she entered a room to begin a day's work, and the blue light would blink again as she left. She would be credited every time she entered a studio to paint part of an upcoming show or entered a museum to help hang exhibits or any of the other tasks available through the Art Guild...or even when she helped out with the little kids at Ladybug Playhouse. Her web was connected to Art Pod's computer system which tallied the hours and sent them to Western Division. When she used credits in other places, Western Division would be notified, and they would send goods in exchange. A computer catalogue kept a running total of current surplus goods to be used in these exchanges.

There was very much an honor system at work, too. Cleo would only need to touch a spot near her ring finger to deactivate the system, for those times when she entered an area but not to work. Nobody cheated because that created a cloudy energy around you that everyone else could feel, and some could even see.

Cleo had learned that in the olden days you had to be at least eighteen years and sometimes twenty-one years old before you would be allowed to go wherever you wanted on your own. This was because there was so much violence in the old world. Parents were afraid of their children getting hurt, so they kept them at home as long as possible.

Then the change had come. This was what Bee, Cleo's Past Class teacher, had called "the quantum leap of consciousness." Many claimed it was a miracle. Almost overnight people started looking at each other differently. They began forgiving each other and themselves, too, when they made a mistake.

Old trapped air was leaking out of the balloon of hate, and there was nothing left to sustain it. It was as if the air itself had changed, and everyone was breathing something new. All people everywhere began to feel a connection with everyone else.

Around the world wars ground to a halt. The first to end was the seemingly endless war between Israel and Palestine. Within days fighting in other Middle Eastern countries stopped as enemies put down their weapons and really looked at each other for the first time. Then the civil wars raging in Africa ended. It was as if everyone in the whole world had dropped quite suddenly out of a very bad dream. People were stunned.

Soon a feeling of pure joy rushed in to fill the void. There was relief and laughter and hugging as long lost brothers and sisters who had been enemies the week before moved through their bombed out cities and towns to begin the massive clean up efforts. At night all over the world there was dancing in the streets. By day guns and other weapons were gathered and tossed into piles to be disassembled and the metal smelted down for new building supports.

Finally the earth itself gave a big sigh of relief. At least that's the way Cleo liked to think of it.

Laughing, Cleo held her hand up to her face again and ran towards the dorm to show off her new status to her best friend Mage, who had promised to wait. She would be one of the honored graduates at a fine celebration this weekend!

~ Chapter 2 ~

Excitement was high in the quad that housed the Artists' Guild. All students who had turned fourteen within the last year and who carried the light webbing which showed their new journey status were being honored this weekend. This was the first step to adulthood, to one day being a full fledged artist or teacher or gallery director and living in the adult wing of the pod with most of the other grown-ups.

Jeori sat in his small room looking out his window at the flurry of comings and goings across the Quad. For now he felt happy just to be here. He could wait for journey status and all that came with it...except for maybe one thing.

Jeori's thoughts swung to the first day when he had stepped off Air Transit and was met by an older student named Ron who would drive him to his new home. As they made their way to the fleet of two-person Veet Cars housed in the parking garage, Ron had proudly showed off the newly placed webbing beneath the skin of his right hand.

"You mean you're only fourteen and already *driving*?" Jeori had asked, hurrying to keep up with the long-legged boy.

"Sure, that's a part of journey status," Ron had replied happily. "And driving is totally safe. Remember that the Veets have force field buffers that activate when they are moving, so it is impossible to get hurt or to hurt someone else on the road." As they entered the garage Jeori noticed a yellow light flash through the skin of Ron's hand. He looked up to see rows of mini cars in all the colors of the rainbow. Ron led the younger boy to one of the lime green models, and they climbed in. Ron put the car in manual overdrive and took off driving fast.

The teenager kept chattering all fifteen minutes to Art Pod—about his current projects, his friends, and some class called Interdimensional Travel that he particularly liked. As they pulled to a stop in front of the Artists' Guild, the older boy opened the passenger door remotely and impatiently motioned Jeori out. He said "See you 'round" and took off leaving the nervous ten-year-old to face the big double doors alone.

Taking a deep breath Jeori had walked forward to ring the bell. Without warning the large doors swung open. An old woman stood before him. She had smiling eyes, long gray hair, and she wore a flowered artist's smock over blue jeans.

"Welcome home, Jeori," the old woman said in a kindly voice. "We're so very glad you've decided to join us here at Art Pod. My name is Leah Smith, but around here I'm called Grandma Leah." At this point Grandma Leah had given him a great hug. Leah was the official grandma for his wing and so was the first to greet him. Then he met Grandpa Stanley from the next wing over and Grandma Theresa and then three of the second year students. He got hugs from all of them.

Jeori smiled at the memory. It had been a nice way to begin after feeling nervous about coming here. It was good to know that whenever you needed someone older to talk to or just comfort and hugs, the many grandpas and grandmas of Art Pod would be ready with arms open wide.

Next, one of the older students had led Jeori up the winding staircase to this room on the second floor.

A beginning set of clothes had been carefully laid out on the single bed. There was a backpack sporting the Artists' Guild logo on the front pocket, a flip phone and a "comp" (personal compact computer) on the small desk—also a sketchbook, a small set of water colors, a pad of thick water color paper, and a diary for journaling—as well as his class and lunch schedule. The student had shown him the cabinet of clean clothes and the bathroom at the end of the hall.

Jeori had been putting away the last of his clothes in the small set of drawers when he'd heard a knock on his door. "Hi, Jeori, I'm your new neighbor. Can I come in?" That was the first time he had met the bright, red-headed girl named Kayla. And now in just a few short weeks they were already fast friends.

~ Chapter 3 ~

The two girls stepped off the earthen path and onto the red carpeted runway which led into The Closet. The moment that their feet touched the carpet, the large brass door began to swing silently inward.

Cleo's eyes swept the insides of the enormous building. A good number of teenagers and adults and a few children were at the racks trying to find outfits for tomorrow's festivities. Cleo recognized some of her pod mates in the crowd.

The girl shook her head in wonder. How lucky she felt to be part of the same quad that housed Fiber Arts West. All the newest styles of clothing in every color and fabric could be found here at The Closet to be borrowed and then returned. Some of these clothes had probably been on display for less than a week. There was also a large section of shoes, replicas of antique clothing, and exotic costumes for the seasonal costume parties held throughout the year. And of course the seamstresses and machines of Fiber Arts provided the everyday student wear for her pod as well; the artist smocks, pants, tee shirts, sweatshirts, coats, underwear, swimsuits, pajamas, and footwear.

"Come on!" said Mage breaking into her friend's thoughts. "We've got two hours total to choose and get back to the pod, and we still have to get jewelry." Mage pulled Cleo towards the Juniors Section. An hour later after returning their discarded choices to the racks, both girls had chosen an outfit for Cleo's coming of age party and had found "good for dancing" shoes to match.

On their way out a yellow light flashed under Cleo's skin to mark the "borrow" she had just made. Since her best friend had yet to reach the golden age of fourteen, Mage had to stop and give her name and pod assignment to the attendant.

The friends rushed down the path carrying their large dress boxes. Inside the Quad Jewelry Exchange they deposited their boxes by the door and quickly lost track of time trying on nearly every bracelet, necklace, and pair of earrings on display. Cleo was so excited when she spotted the heart shaped blue topaz pendant surrounded by small diamonds. It would be a perfect match for the flowing aqua-colored silk dress she had chosen. Simple gold hoop earrings would complete her outfit. Mage borrowed a delicate emerald and diamond ring with matching drop earrings. These she knew would look great with the deep green satin tunic and matching tights she would wear.

Yikes! We're late! Cleo thought. The girls allowed their information to be recorded for the "borrow." They took the small black velvet bags holding the jewelry, picked up their clothing boxes, and sprinted back to Art Pod. Dropping their selections in their rooms, they ran down the stairs, both reaching the cafeteria just as the final dinner bell rang.

~ ~ ~

As Cleo licked the last of the apple strudel and whipped cream from her spoon, her thoughts turned to her mother and father. They would each be arriving early tomorrow morning to enjoy some special time with their daughter before the afternoon ceremony and the dinner and dancing afterward. To save time they had each planned to teleport to Art Pod directly rather than to travel part way by Air Transit. Cleo's mother was coming from her Biology Quad on the East Coast and her father from the Physical Anthropology Pod in Northern China where he was a visiting scientist.

With so many relatives porting in from everywhere on Earth, Cleo's parents had needed to schedule the exact time and the exact location on the grid where they each would be appearing so there could be no possible collisions. And Cleo would be there to greet them.

~ Chapter 4 ~

Wake up, Jeori, said the sweet and familiar voice in the center of his head.

Thanks, Anabadezia, Jeori thought back and yawned. *You sure are good at waking me up.* He turned back over for just five more minutes sleep.

The voice of his guardian angel spoke again. *Did you forget your field trip, Child?*

Oh, you're right. I'm up! Jeori said aloud and threw back the covers. This was one day he didn't want to be late for breakfast. Today his activity group, comprised of twenty first year Art Pod students, was going to tour San Francisco. Jeori had taken a short tour of the city last year with his parents. But that trip had been in the middle of visits to all the different pods, and he'd been so busy trying to decide where he wanted to end up that he was distracted. This time he wanted to really pay attention...to really take it all in.

Jeori zipped his jeans and pulled the new tangerine colored tee shirt over his head. It was this year's standard pod shirt with the Artists' Guild logo at the chest. Decorating the back was the print of an abstract painting created by second year student Jonas Dobbs. *Maybe the painting I'm finishing now will be chosen for next year's official tee,* Jeori thought. He sent the wish skyward as he tucked the shirt into his jeans and headed out the door.

The boy washed up quickly, pulled his shoulder-length auburn hair into a ponytail, and rushed downstairs to the cafeteria. He located the section for his activity group by the excited voices and by the students' matching shirts. Jeori sat down at one of the two tables next to a boy he knew.

Each activity group was named after something in nature. For first year students it was fruit. Jeori's group was Tangerines, while Kayla's group was Apples and so on. The second year activity groups were named for animals and the third for gemstones.

This was Tangerine's first field trip together so just before breakfast was brought out everyone introduced themselves. Today's menu was one of Jeori's favorites... buttermilk waffles, scrambled eggs, and orange juice. However this day in his excitement the ten-year-old would pay little attention to what or how fast he ate.

Jeori placed a gob of eggs on his plate and then a waffle, drowned his waffle in maple syrup, grabbed his fork, and dug right in. He finished his meal in a record two minutes twenty-three seconds, his last gulp of juice punctuated by a loud and rather painful maple-flavored burp.

To his right Jake chuckled. To his left Marcus said "Excuse you!" But Michiko, the girl sitting directly across from Jeori, had a different reaction. She smiled and nodded with approval. "I bet you didn't know," she said in a clear voice, "that in Japan burping after a meal was considered a supreme compliment to the chef for his fine cooking."

At these encouraging words belches began erupting around the table as each boy tried to outdo the one next to him. While Michiko looked embarrassed that she had said anything, the other girls at the table rolled their eyes and shook their heads. With the contest in full swing, no one at first noticed the change in energy.

Jeori was the first to look up. His face immediately turned three shades of red. The prettiest teacher in school, *his* painting teacher, was standing at the head of the table with a half smile on her face. She waited patiently, and as she waited she played with the ends of her long blond hair.

"Guys...." Jeori began. One by one the other student followed his eyes.

Like an exploding cannon ball came the final and the loudest belch of all. It was set off by one Igor Nudleman..."Noodle" to his friends. His blue eyes gleamed proudly in his round face as he checked for reactions to this prize winner. All was deathly quiet. A few students cocked their heads meaningfully from Igor toward the head of the table.

The eleven-year-old looked quickly in that direction and mouthed "O." He grabbed his napkin and delicately wiped his syrupy lips. Then he forced a big smile. "Err...uh...hi there, teacher. I was just complimenting the chef!"

"So I hear," the young professor replied, biting her lower lip to keep from laughing. "And that last one was quite the biggest compliment of the morning."

Jeori shook his head. *How long has she been standing there?*

"For those of you I haven't met, my name is Lydia Crawford. You may call me Lydia. I teach many of the first and second year painting classes and also drawing here at Art Pod. I recognize some of you from my beginning painting class. Good morning, Amethyst! Hi, Jeori! And hola, Juan!

"San Francisco is one of my favorite destinations," the young professor continued. "Therefore I arranged for an intern to watch over my classes so that I could join you on your field trip today. Don Gierno, who teaches ceramics, will accompany the other half of the Tangerines." She nodded toward the next table where Professor Gierno was speaking.

"The Veet van is already waiting out front," she continued. "You have five minutes for the lavatories. Our weather forecast today is mostly clear but cool with patchy morning fog. So be sure to pick a jacket of the right size from the main hall closet on our way out. We will travel a short distance by van and then meet the small bubble crafts for the rest of our adventure. For those of you who haven't bubbled yet...well, the word fun doesn't half cover it."

~ ~ ~

Minutes later the Tangerines and their chaperones were under way. As promised the van reached its destination in no time. Two multi-use bubble craft waited on the large round landing pad. Each oblong vehicle was formed by a series of three glass-like bubbles for clear viewing on sides, top, and bottom. The fourteen seats in each bubble appeared to float on the clear surface of the "floor."

As his teacher and the last of the ten students in his group got settled, Jeori noticed something different about his seat from the one he'd used during the first trip with his parents. There were two sets of vertical slots, one at shoulder and one at waist level. He tried to force his finger into one of the slots in his seat back. It didn't fit.

"Greetings, Adventurers!" boomed the voice of the tall, uniformed black man who had suddenly appeared at the front of the first row of seats. "My name is Captain George Rifkin." He tipped his sky blue captain's cap. "You may call me Captain George. Today you fine students of Art Pod are in for a rare treat given only to the lucky few! Prepare yourself to experience the Deluxe Bubble Tour.

"With our fine bubble craft, it is always safety first. So please put your arms out in front of you at chest level, like this." The students followed his example. Instantly metal bands slid smoothly from the slots Jeori had noticed. The bands locked together forming a strong harness over each passenger. Captain George smiled mildly. "Don't be at all concerned about these restraints. We will be traveling at various speeds and elevations and from time to time today we will be doing some fast and, if I do say so, some rather splendid maneuvering. So it is vitally important that you be secure."

"My drive control is behind me in the front cabin," the Captain continued. "I will speak to you as we go. I will also be able to hear you to answer any questions you may have. Is everyone ready?" Without waiting for an answer he turned and disappeared through the cabin door.

Excited smiles lit the faces of every student... except one. Ten-year-old Amethyst, a short, chubby girl known for her clairvoyance, was looking clearly unhappy. She wiggled in her harness. Lydia, who was sitting next to the girl, patted her hand and gave her a reassuring smile. "Don't worry," she said. "It will be fun."

"No, it *won't*," Amethyst declared.

~ Chapter 5 ~

Without warning the bubble craft began rising silently straight up into the blue sky. Its movement was slow at first and then gradually faster, until it reached an elevation of nearly three thousand feet above sea level. The Bubble hovered soundlessly as the students looked out the sides and down beneath their feet. The view from this elevation was amazing! They began to move horizontally and then lower again for a beginning tour of the region. Jeori's gaze moved east to the hills and to the valley beyond where he had lived with his mom and dad. The houses from this distance were just small spots.

In moments the bubble craft was circling above the quad containing the sprawling three-tiered concrete and glass building that the members of Art Pod called home. A hallway connected their building to the locker rooms and to the Olympic-sized indoor swimming pool, which was used for classes and free swim by everyone in the quad. Behind the Artists' Guild building was a building housing the main art gallery and beside that a second smaller one.

The Actors' Guild stood directly across from Art Pod. At the front were two three-storied long rectangular buildings with a courtyard between. These held the classrooms and living areas for the junior actors. The entrance to one building resembled the prow of a pirate ship. And the entrance to the second resembled the aft of the ship. Beside this was performance hall, which held the main auditorium plus several smaller arenas for the many plays and skits put on by the guild. Continuing the pirate theme, the roof of Performance Hall was shaped like a pirate's three-cornered hat. Behind and at an angle stood the two buildings which housed the adult classrooms and living quarters.

Between the art and acting pods sat the four matching shingled roofed buildings of Fiber Arts West, and behind these stood the smaller square building that housed The Closet. A curved path led from The Closet to the Western Jewelry Exchange. The fourth major building in the quad, the domed Healing Arts, was located on the other side of the swimming pool.

The next quad over was not far. It housed Architecture, Community Planning, Cuisine Arts, and the Green Garden Group. A large organic garden, two greenhouses, and a three-storied hydroponics tower provided vegetables, fruits, and flowers for the three closest quads in all seasons. And there were nut trees as well. Beyond these horses, cows, sheep, and goats dotted the fields and sloping hills of Animal Care and Farming Pods.

The bubble craft moved in for a closer view of Art Pod. Everyone pointed and stared at the scene below them trying to pick out their own dorm room windows as they slowly circled. Without warning they lifted high into the morning sky once again, the craft switching to horizontal movement as it made a bee line for the coast. White seagulls winged through the bright sky as they approached the city.

~ ~ ~

The first Jeori noticed of San Francisco was a layer of fog below him with different shapes sticking out of it. There were some rectangles and some squares and was that—Yes! There was the top of the pyramid that Jeori remembered seeing on the trip with his parents.

"Welcome to the city of San Francisco," Captain George Rifkin announced. "With the fog cover today the city looks much as it might have from a low flying plane some seventy years ago. Now let's move in for a closer view."

The bubble craft drew lower toward the city and banked left. "For those of you in my class," Lydia added, "please pay special attention to the scene below us. As we travel around the tops of these buildings, notice the shapes and the play of sun and shadow on those shapes. Our next painting assignment will center on what we are seeing here."

"Moving down...down...and still down." The captain's voice echoed dramatically as they drifted slowly toward the buildings beneath them. Suddenly fog engulfed their craft. They continued sinking slowly until they landed near the pyramid. Jeori was looking between his feet at the moment of the splash.

"Here we are near the top of what was once known as the Transamerica Pyramid," the captain explained. "At eight hundred fifty feet or two hundred sixty meters from ground level, this was at one time the tallest building in San Francisco and one of the two hundred tallest buildings in the entire world. It was designed with this pyramidal shape to survive even catastrophic earthquakes, and as we will see, considering what this city has been through, it has done quite well.

"For those of you who have already taken a trip to San Francisco by bubble, I have a question for you. Where do we want to go next, Crew?"

"Down...down," Jeori and three other students said softly.

2065

"Lou-der! I can't hear you!" intoned the captain.

"Down...down!" yelled all the children.

"Then down it is! Hold onto your seats! We're going down."

The humming of a motor marked the bubble craft's change from force field mode to submarine as it began to descend slowly through the murky water. It moved in a lazy spiral down and around the four-sided pyramid and toward the ocean floor. Jeori noticed that while some windows in the pyramid were still intact, many windows were now open portals. A large school of small fish swam out of one window and sped upward toward the surface, flashing silver.

The bubble craft crept slowly through the business district and city center, meandering through schools of fish, between the once grand Opera House, and the domed building that had been City Hall. The large double row of vertical windows of Symphony Hall were now jagged, broken shards with long, dangling seaweed strips clinging to the edges. The look was of some magical, fluttering curtain. Fish came and went through the seaweed curtain. *Maybe the fish are enjoying a concert in there*, Jeori thought and laughed to himself. The craft made an abrupt u-turn.

"We now move downhill to the area once called the Marina," Captain George announced. He was quiet for a few minutes as the children took in the mostly ruined houses skirting what had once been San Francisco Bay. "Now look ahead through the water. What is that we're fast approaching? Do any of you know?"

Jeori and the other students who'd already toured the city started to respond. But before they could say a word, the captain answered his own question. "Welcome students to the world famous Golden Gate

Bridge. Until about thirty years ago this bridge marked where the Pacific Ocean met San Francisco Bay."

As they reached the submerged bridge, the bubble craft sank quickly to touch the sea floor. Suddenly it angled up diagonally. With no more warning than "Hold on, fun lovers!" craft and passengers lurched forward.

Jeori now realized why they wore the special harnesses, and why Captain George had called this the *deluxe* tour. This was in danger of becoming the best carnival ride ever!

They sped along the length of the bridge weaving between the tipped pillars that had supported the roadway above. At one end of the bridge the curved struts which had once connected sets of cables to the roadway had collapsed. Forty or perhaps fifty cables were now loose and swaying with the tides overhead. With only support on one end, the roadway tipped sharply downward.

"We must be extremely careful now," cautioned the captain in a dramatic voice as they slowly circled. "Those loose, swinging cables could destroy our fine craft in an instant. If even one of them hit us we would be in deep trouble. We would become food for the fish...shark bait, you might say! But never fear you fine students of Art Pod," intoned Captain George. "I have done this before."

Without warning their craft moved into one quick diagonal loop and then another. On the second loop they narrowly missed a whole set of the snaking cables. Jeori reflexively grabbed hold of his armrest, his eyes wide.

There was no comment from the cabin. But once out of the danger zone the captain asked, "Now who wants to slide?" Again without waiting for an answer he maneuvered the bubble to the top of the roadway. He seemed to let go of control. The bubble craft flew down mere inches above the tilted road, the children squealing "e-e-e-e-e!" It hovered a moment at the bottom, then turned back up for another go.

As they made their way slowly up the ramp, Jeori finally had time to notice Dungeness crabs of different sizes walking beneath him on the roadway. Reddish-brown crabs were climbing the towers, too, and a few were even balancing on the swaying cables. The closer he looked the more crabs he saw.

Captain and "crew" spent fifteen minutes more of what the captain had earlier called "fast and rather splendid maneuvering" speeding up, down, and around the fallen bridge. It was fun at first. The captain's voice would boom with enthusiasm. "How do you like *this*?" he would say...or "Let's take another dive, shall we?" And of course Captain George never waited for an answer before doing exactly what he wanted.

By the time they finally slowed down to leave the area, Jeori thought that the other Tangerines near him looked every bit as green and shaky as he felt. And while Lydia Crawford held the girl's brown hair back from her round face, little Amethyst Stone was throwing up in a paper bag.

~ ~ ~

Jeori breathed a sigh of relief as the bubble craft moved into a slower pace to explore the underwater hills and neighborhoods of the closely packed Victorian style houses that had helped make San Francisco famous. He noticed some houses were still in fairly good shape considering the shaking earth and pounding tides, while others had collapsed and were in ruins.

Captain George began speaking again. "Now imagine what it must have been like to live here long before the surging tides forced the residents inland. Imagine the shops and the schools and the playgrounds. Imagine the cars and trucks and buses and cable cars of yore filling the streets over which we glide. Can't you almost hear the horns honking and the sirens going off in the distance? It was a noisy, confusing world back then."

A school of elongated, striped fish swam the length of the Bubble and angled upward. "What is *that*?" Jeori asked and pointed to a large, nearly intact Victorian house on his right. Something was swimming toward them through an open doorway. The something was grey on top and white on the bottom and...really big. "It's a shark!" he exclaimed.

"Ah, yes! The young man is quite correct," the Captain remarked in a serious tone. "And this is not just *any* shark, but one of the most dangerous creatures of the sea, a Great White Shark. Notice the five handsome striped bass swimming directly above us now. I do believe our Great White has just spotted his lunch."

With a whip of his powerful tail the shark sped upward, opened his jaws, snapped his sharp teeth, and bit the nearest fish in half. He quickly gobbled up the remains. A missed piece of the fish landed on the top of the bubble right above Jeori. The shark flashed down and bumped the clear roof to grab the last morsel just as the startled boy looked up...and right into the shark's open mouth.

Blackness closed in. Ten-year-old Jeori Kellogg had fainted.

2065

Jeori's Journal

Yesterday was probably the weirdest day of my life. I don't know if my teacher, Lydia, was there when I let go of the burp that started that STUPID contest. I sure hope not. But she was right there after I fainted. She's the one who woke me up by holding some smelly stuff under my nose.

I guess nobody noticed that I blacked out at first. So I missed the last part of the tour. The other kids told me later—the part when Captain George told the old story about the beginning of the guild system, and the five friends who were forced to leave San Francisco after the waters surrounded their houses. But I remember the story....

So one woman who had lots and lots of money asked her friends to come with her, and she promised they would build a nice new house just for them on her big piece of land far, far away. But one friend was a school teacher and one friend worked with getting housing for poor people and one friend was an architect and one was—I forget the last one. Anyway,...they thought maybe they could try something different. And they got the idea for a place you could live and study and share and maybe not have to use money anymore after they got it set up. They asked more people to come help and figure out how to do it.

So the rich woman took all of her money out of the bang—no, that's bank—*every single last quarter... to start building and putting everything together. All her fancy jewelry started the first jewelry exchange, and her fancy clothes started the first closet, so that anyone could wear them to parties if they were the same size as her. And then her friends put in everything they had, too. And then other people joined, and they did the same thing.*

They put solar cells all over their roofs—and set up wind turbines nearby, too—so they had lots and lots of energy to keep warm and turn on the lights and for whatever else they needed. This was called being off the grill—I guess because they cooked their own energy.

They planted a big garden so they could eat what they grew themselves. Oh! And there's the part about the rancher who had the land next to them, and how they became friends and shared their extra energy with him. And then he decided to form his own pod that connected with theirs!

So when everything else was ready they set up the school part. They named their pod Community Planning, and it was the first. Then they did outreach to show other people how to set up pods of their own. Anyway, I already knew all this stuff from Past Class, so I sure didn't need to hear it again from crazy Captain George.

The weirdest part of that old story is my most favortist part. At the same time the five friends were thinking up the idea here, another group in England came up with the very same thing after they had to move inland, too, because of their ocean. And the two groups had never even talked to each other!

The teachers say that there are these little invisible lines of light that connect all people everywhere, and that these lines of light go out in another dimension and into this great big web that connects us with spirit, too. So this is how people living on different parts of the Earth can get the same exact idea at the same exact instant.

But what I like to think is that these people's angels were all friends in another world, and that the angels whispered the idea into the minds of the women in Amerada (I guess it was called America then) and into the minds of those people in England at the very same time.

Some people don't hear their angels. I'm sure glad I do. Anabadezia is really nice. If I'm sad and I ask her to, she covers me in light and a minute later I feel all better!

~ Chapter 6 ~

Cleo ran up and wrapped her arms around her best friend, waves of excitement rippling off her slim body.

"I'm in!" she exclaimed. "I can't believe it, Mage! I got the student exchange. China, here I come!" The fourteen-year-old raised her arms and pumped them in the air.

Mage took a deep breath and stepped back running a hand through her short, wavy brown hair. Her freckled face didn't appear particularly happy. "So when do you leave?"

"Only four months from now in mid-March!" Cleo gushed. "And I'll get to visit my dad, too, and tour his university! Aren't you excited for me, Mage?"

There was a moment of silence. "Six months is a long time."

"Yeah, I know. But we can still talk by vid. And you'll have Li Ha to get to know. She seems really nice. I'll introduce you onscreen. You won't mind helping her...showing her around, introducing her to our friends, and getting her to my classes at first, will you?"

Mage took another breath and tried to block her thoughts. What choice did she have in this whole thing anyway?

"There's just so much to do," Cleo gushed before her friend had a chance to say anything. "I didn't know if I could get it, so I've barely started learning Mandarin...and...and...."

"Don't implode. You've got plenty of time. Just keep the learning tabs in your ears at night."

"But I have to *practice*, too."

"You can practice on me, all right? It will be fun," Mage said beginning to accept that this was really happening. "English is the Earth Standard now, so you don't have to know *everything*."

"Yeah, but I need to know enough not to seem rude."

"Right...so tell me about it," Mage said as they made their way to one of the central quad benches. "You're only beginning journey status, and I know a bunch of older students applied for the China exchange this semester, too. I'm not saying your art isn't fine. It is. But what happened?"

"Well, you know that whenever there's a student exchange with another part of the world, each student has to have something special to teach that the other pod will be interested in learning." Mage nodded. "In my essay I shared the painting method I came up with, about how I concentrate on an emotion and put it into every color of paint I'm about to put on the canvas. So maybe I'll put excitement into a shade of yellow or sadness into mint green paint. Then as I blend on the canvas I let the impressions come in from the emotions and that forms sort of a story. Usually there are symbols that show up, and they help tell the story, too. So I begin with just feelings for each color. But I don't know what the painting will be, do I? So it almost forms itself.

"See, traditional Chinese painting is just the opposite. I studied up. Each painting is carefully planned and carried out following certain set rules about style and balance between the elements. Traditional Chinese painting comes from the mind, but at the end you feel the emotion that the artist planned for you to feel. I start with emotions, and they form the story which becomes mind food. Those are the words I used...*mind food*. I think the judges liked that."

"And you sent photos of the three paintings that I helped you pick, Cleo. I remember."

"Yeah, and one more, too! Then I got the idea for each of the judges to write down the stories that they felt from the paintings, but not to tell each other what they got until after they were all done. Then they could compare their stories. They used different words, but their stories were really similar to each other and close to the stories I got, too! I bet they thought that would be a fun experiment for their students."

"I can see why they picked you, Cleo...my brilliant Cleo!" Mage's smile was genuine as was the hug she gave her best friend. "So answer me this. How will you get all the way to China?"

"I'm teleporting."

There was sudden panic in Mage's voice as she replied, "No...no, that's not possible. They can't let you, Cleo. You're just finishing first level teleportation this semester. You've only practiced porting from one side of the field to the other, for goodness sakes. If you lost your concentration you could end up in the middle of the *ocean* or something!"

"But you see...I won't be alone."

"You'll be piggy backing. But who with?"

"This is the best part. I won't be piggy backing, but piggy *fronting* with Stefan Zuniga. He'll be hugging me!"

"Yikes!" Mage exclaimed squeezing her eyes tight. "The hottest teacher on the planet is hugging my best friend all the way to China. I can't sta-a-nd it!"

"And all the way back. It'll probably take a total of twenty seconds, so don't get *too* excited."

"But I am. I *am* really excited for you now, Cleo. Just send lots of vids of the Art Pod and your new friends so I feel like I'm there, too...okay?"

"You got it. Yikes! Look at the time! Games class starts in five minutes. Let's not be late again." Cleo pulled Mage to standing, and the two friends raced for class.

~ Chapter 7 ~

Mage and Cleo pulled opened the door of Games Creation and hurried inside. As expected, Scarecrow was watching.

The name "Scarecrow" was given to Professor Andrew Jacks by a disgruntled student weeks ago, and it had spread around Art Pod like lightening. Jacks did resemble a scarecrow. That's all there was to it. He had dirty blonde hair which stuck out at odd angles and beady eyes that looked as if they had been placed too close together on his narrow face. Also, his teachers' standard clothing comprised of tan slacks and a blue shirt was several sizes too large for his thin frame. Cleo's personal theory was that he balled up his clothing and sat on it every evening to have all the wrinkles in place for the next day.

The girls rushed to take the two remaining places at different work tables just as the bell rang. Cleo knew what would come next.

"It's so nice to see that you ladies have managed to join us an entire second before the final bell," Professor Jacks said with his usual touch of sarcasm. He sighed loudly. "A minute or two early would be a nice treat, but it is something I have not come to expect from the two of you."

What is it with him? Cleo thought looking down at her desk top. *He's getting worse with every class.*

"Now," Professor Jacks said shifting his attention. "I assume that you have each completed not only your game plan, but your first trial-ready game. Is everyone with me thus far?" All fifteen students nodded. "I'm ecstatic," he said flatly.

"What I'd like you to do is to...quietly please... share your game plan with the student directly across from you. Explain to him or to her the rules of play and let them have at it for a few minutes. Then switch. This way you may each get a feeling for the absolute *brilliance* of each other's games.

"Finally, constructive criticisms will be in order. What could this game master do to create either more complexity, more interest or if called for, more clarity in their game? Since we are an uneven number, I will be looking over Milo's game with him today."

Cleo felt the silent groan from Milo. She shook her head at the barely concealed rage in her teacher's voice and took a deep breath. Then she placed her comp notebook on the table, opened the lid, and quietly said "game" to bring it up onto the screen. Only then did she look up to discover her partner for the day.

Surprise shot through Cleo as the grey, unreadable eyes of Kadrun Connelly met hers. Kad Connelly was the mystery man of Art Pod. He was tall and Cleo thought good looking, though he seemed not to know it or care. He wore his jet black hair slicked back, though a few loose strands always curled at his forehead. Daily Kadrun ghosted through the halls. He sat in the back of his classrooms, did his studio work quietly, and then disappeared. When he made it to the cafeteria he ate alone, even if there were other students at his table. And he always wore black. For this reason the students of Art Pod had started calling him "Mr. Black"...but never, *never* to his face.

Beautiful eyes, Cleo thought and was immediately embarrassed that the thought had leaked out. Had he heard her thought? His eyes did seem to grow darker for a moment. And was that a hint of a smile? Cleo blushed.

"I suppose we should get to this before Scarecrow gets on your case again," Kad said in a surprisingly deep voice for fourteen. "Do you want to play my game first? It's for two people so we'll have to play together."

Cleo was not at all surprised that Kadrun's game concerned two skeletons or that the game board was mostly black and the skeletons perfectly drawn. That was entirely to be expected. But she *was* surprised that his game was so dull. She never thought of Kadrun as dull...just unknown, unknowable, and maybe just a little dangerous, though she couldn't say why.

Kad's was a standard board game, and the rules were simple. Get the gray skeleton home to the cemetery from his starting place under the bare-limbed tree in the upper left quadrant, through the darkness, and to the coffin, bottom right, while your opponent tries to get there first with his red skeleton. There was the expected spinner to show how many jumps you got.

They played a game and Cleo won. She looked up. What could she say? To her surprise what she came up with was, "Why did you choose this as your elective if you hate games so much?"

Kad looked into her green eyes and shrugged. "Maybe I don't. So what would you do with it, Elf?"

"You think I'm an elf?"

"That's my best guess."

Cleo was secretly thrilled. She gave Kad a few ideas for his game—some simple, some complex. She liked the computer game idea she came up with the best, but then she was really into comp games, especially

3D ones, and there wasn't time in the semester for him to try what she suggested. But she did come up with improvements. And he listened.

Kadrun found Cleo's computer game fast-paced, interesting, and full of light—though he didn't tell her that last part. *She's sunshine to my darkness*, he suddenly realized. Kad looked down at the table and quickly blocked this thought like so many others behind the high walls of his mind.

Cleo's Diary

I don't write in you much, do I, diary? But this week I had two things happen that I didn't expect, and I want to get them down. The first is I got the China exchange! I can hardly believe it. I leave March thirteenth! There were five of my pod mates that applied. And I'm the youngest. It's exciting, but it's kind of scary, too. Mage says I'll do great. I hope she's right.

The other thing...Professor Jacks is gone. This is what happened. Mage and I walked into Games class this afternoon...late as usual, but only by a minute. I knew it wouldn't matter anyway. If we were on time for a whole week, he'd still find something sarcastic to say. "You girls made it on time. Yippee," or "Seven days in a row on time. Get out the halos." Anyway, we rushed in and found seats. The class was full but weirdly—no Scarecrow. Everyone waited a few minutes. Then we took out our games and started working.

Kad came over to show me the improvements he'd made since last class. He added a "Go Back to Beginning" component, and he made some stations on the way with instructions...nothing new in the world of gaming, but better.

Maybe he just wanted to show it to me. Maybe there could be something else. When he called me "Elf" last time something happened—like a crack in his shell—like a small flower pushing up in a space between stones. But then he closed up again. Does he like me?

Anyway, a fifth level apprentice showed up and told us Professor Jacks had left to join a mathematics pod somewhere in Europe, and that she would be taking over our class for the rest of the semester. Hooray!

I feel kind of sorry for Scarecrow now. Maybe someone broke his heart. Maybe someone told him he was a bad teacher. Whatever it was, the energy in the room sure changed the second we all learned he wouldn't be back. It was like a heater coming on when you're freezing or the rain stopping and the sun coming out.

~ Chapter 8 ~

The sky was overcast, and a cold chill bit the early November air as Kadrun Connelly made his way toward the benches near the center of the quad. He shivered and pulled up the hood of the fleece-lined jacket he'd grabbed on his way out of Art Pod.

Kad looked around and sighed. The area between the pods was mostly empty this afternoon, which was just the way he wanted it. He would deal with the cold. Sometimes being around his pod mates was overwhelming. It just reminded him of how different he was...of how much he didn't fit in. He flashed on the petite, spiky-haired girl he'd been working with in Games for the last two periods. *You're way out of my league, Cleo.* He sighed again.

The teenager turned slowly in a circle looking closely at the buildings surrounding him. He thought, *yes, there,* and chose a bench facing the two long Actors' Pod buildings. The latest assignment in his advanced drawing class was to sketch a structure in the quad using perspective and then render it accurately in pen and ink with any surrounding foliage. He took out his sketchbook, pencil, eraser, and ruler and began. In minutes the two buildings were taking shape.

Kad's focus was good, and he hardly needed to use his eraser this time. He remembered the first times he'd been asked to use perspective in Lydia's beginning drawing class. It had been so confusing trying to get the angles right or even to make his lines straight at first, and he had made loads of mistakes. *The way it is with anything new,* he thought.

Kadrun glanced up when someone sat down on the other end of his bench. The fourteen-year-old planned to ignore the newcomer and began to draw the next line. He looked over again. The grizzled old man just sat there staring at nothing. But his thoughts were crazy. Kad saw flashes of concrete walls and steel bars and a vicious fight in what looked like a cafeteria. There was yelling and a knife and blood.

"Who are you?" Kad breathed. He shivered. Had he said that out loud?

"Excuse me?" said the man turning his head to stare at the black clad teenager.

"I'm sorry, I...." Kad didn't know what else to say.

"Ah, you're one of them telepaths. Not a pretty sight, is it?"

Kad thought momentarily about lying to the old man and pretending he hadn't seen anything, but what was the use? "I don't understand what I saw," he answered simply.

"Well, let's start at the beginning. My name's John...John Willets. I'm fairly new to Art Pod...just been here since September.

"And I'm Kad Connelly." He held up his sketchbook. "I'm with Art Pod, too. But of course I'm in the Young Students' wing. So what was all of that?"

"Before the change I was a lifer over at Folsom State Prison. For a moment I was just rememberin' what it was like in the old days. Didn't know you'd be lookin' in."

The teenager started to apologize. "Nah...think nothing of it, boy. I got over bein' sensitive long ago. In all my years I must have seen everything up there at the prison. It might seem strange to you, but I'm out here in the cold just now to get a little space. It's hard to get used to pod life. Everybody's just so darned ...."

"Happy," Kad finished

"Yeah, or you could say *bouncy, busy,* or *noisy.* Take yer pick."

Kad shook his head. "I know what you mean. Sometimes I feel I can hardly breathe in there. Uh, about the telepathy.... It's kind of a secret. Can we keep this just between us?"

"Sure...nothing' simpler. I would have been dead ten times over if I didn't know how to keep a secret. I can block my thoughts, too...if I concentrate."

The teenager nodded. "But I don't get it," he said scratching his head. "The prisons were closed years ago...long before I was even born. Where have you been all this time?"

"Properly, kid, you could say the prisons were opened. Do you have time for a story?"

Kadrun looked into the man's tired eyes and nodded. "Something drew me out here today. I think maybe it was meeting you. You said you were a *lifer.* What's a lifer?"

"Ah, you young ones have no idea. And that can only be good. You sure you're ready for this?" Kad nodded again.

"Okey dokey!" The old man took a ragged breath. "I was born near the end of the last century in the year of 1990 in the great state of Arkansas in the good old U. S. of A. That was before we linked up with Canada and the name changed. Anyway, my childhood was okay. We was poor, but so was everybody else around us. We made do.

"By the time I hit teenage, my pap had a sickness in his lungs from years working in that darned chicken factory. He got real bad and was laid up in the hospital. The insurance company Mama and Pap had been payin' into for years made up some lame excuse and denied his claim. He died. And just like that all the savings money was wiped out, what with the doctor and the hospital and the funeral parlor to pay. There was nothing else to do, so Mama and me moved out west to live with her sister.

"When my trouble started I was probably a little older than you are now. Sixteen years I was, and none too smart. The neighborhood we moved into was mighty poor. You see we'd gone from country poor to city poor, and in the city there was every kind of crime from purse snatchin' to lots worse. I found out quick that to be safe you had to get protection. And the only way to do that was to join in a gang. So I kept asking this gang of kids near my age if I could join up with 'em. But I was just a country hick to them, and they kept sayin' no and no and no again.

"Finally they dared me to kill this kid one of them was having an argument with. They said they'd let me in if I done it. I don't think they expected me to follow through. They just wanted me off their backs. But stupid me, I took it serious. Short of it is that I got the gun that was my pap's gun, and I *did* shoot the kid. I meant to just injure him...figured they'd let me in anyway if I went that far. But I missed. I got caught real fast. Then I was tried in a court of law as an adult, and sent to prison."

"You mean he died?"

"Yep. My *miss* got that poor kid straight through his heart.

"I figured then and there that was the end of my life. After what I'd done the guilt came rushin' on in, and I thought I should die. But instead the judge said he was settin' an example, and he sentenced me to life in prison. That's what *lifer* means, kid, someone sentenced to spend their whole life behind bars.

"And somehow I survived to see it all. And I do mean all. You got a picture of what it was like before, so I'll squeeze that part of the story in between the folds and skip right ahead.

"You're too young to remember the day that everything changed, but it's branded into my memory like it was yesterday." The old man sat staring at nothing again.

"Do you mind telling me in words?" Kad asked.

"Oh, yeah. Sorry about that. Where was I? Oh, yeah.... So I was lyin' in my bunk one afternoon. I was just driftin' in and out like I did every afternoon. It was February of 2030, I believe...when all of the sudden I felt something huge hit me. It was like a blast of warmth and sweetness and acceptance all rolled up into one. It was the darndest feeling. I could feel a connection with everything and everyone like all over the world. It was grace that hit me, pure and simple... and it hit me *hard*.

"As I lay there I just started bawlin.' Tears was streamin' down my face. I couldn't help myself. For the longest time, I just cried and cried. I finally run out of tears. Then I heard it. All over the cell block everybody else was bawlin', too. Even the roughest of the bunch was cryin' their eyes out.

"Then I'll never forget the sound I heard next. There was the loud click that meant my cell door was gonna open. Then the bars slid back. All down the row I could hear the same thing happenin'. Someone was settin' us free! I stuck my head out into the hallway. Some of the men were high-five'n each other, and some were pushin' through the crowd just hurryin' as fast as they could to get out before whoever done it changed their mind.

"I was shook let me tell you. I'd been in Folsom Prison nearly twenty years by then. I went back into my cell. I lay down on my bunk and turned toward the wall."

"You didn't leave?" Kad asked.

"See, since I was a teenager that prison was the only life I'd known, and I was gettin' on old. My family was long dead. What was I supposed to do as a free man?

"After I thought everybody was gone, I walked out of my cell and through every open door to the front of the prison. The main door was open wide. The prison gate was open wide, too, and then there was the big wide world out there and all that blue sky.

"So I went right back in and over to the kitchen to see what I could find to eat. All that cryin' had worked me up a powerful appetite. I found some others who hadn't left—there was fifteen or so of us—and we had ourselves a dinner party. Bill—he became a good friend after that—Bill had been a cook at a restaurant once. He cooked us up a real feast with the warden's special stash of food."

Kadrun shook his head. "So you stayed. But the food must have run out after awhile."

"Yep, and then providence struck. Some months in and just as our supplies was runnin' low, some people come to see about tearing down the prison. Were they surprised when they found us living there! By then there was only nine of us left. We worked out that we would help with whatever they needed done in exchange for seeds to get a garden goin' and food and clothes and whatever else we needed. There was some talent between us, and we got a good barter system going with those folks that served us many years."

Kad shook his head "Did you say years?"

"Yep, over thirty, if you can believe. Oh, we bartered for some comfortable beds and other things to set the place up better to suit us. And we ventured out now and then. We did okay. It was home.

"Over the years more of my cellmates took off or died. Finally the time came when Bill and me was the only ones left at the old place. Then one day when we was out diggin' in the garden, just like that my dear old friend Bill dropped dead. I borrowed a tractor to dig up a plot to bury him.

"After that was done I figured there was no point stayin' around. I knew about the pods of course 'cause we ended up trading services with several of 'em. I thought back to when I was a kid and how much I liked to draw piturs. I was pretty good, too. The old truck we used to have died years before. So I walked all the way here. And none of the artists turned me away."

"Of course they didn't. Have you written this down, John?" The old man shook his head. "You really should. It feels like an important story."

"I'm not too good with writin', kid, and besides, I'm not ready to share with everybody just yet. What did you say your name was agin?"

"My name is Kad, Kadrun Connelly."

"Do I know that name? Oh, yeah, I do. You got some paintings over in the big gallery, don't ya?" Kad nodded. "I like 'em...real straight and honest. They speak right at me. Well, I'll tell you what Kad Kadrun. You have my permission to tell my story one day if you ever get the urge to...only *after* I'm dead. It shouldn't be too long of a wait on that one."

John rubbed a hand across his scruffy beard and stood. "Will you just look at the hour? It's paintin' time for me. It was nice talking to you, Kad." Without another word former inmate John Willets got up and hobbled away.

Kadrun watched him go. Then realizing his butt was freezing from sitting on the stone bench for so long, he packed up his drawing supplies and headed back to the noise and the warmth of the Artists' Guild.

~ Chapter 9 ~

Electricity ran through the halls and studios of Art Pod as the Season of Lights fast approached. The first celebration, Thanksgiving, was only two days away. Pod mates of all ages ran to and fro with armfuls of decorations, fresh flowers from the greenhouses at Green Garden, and foods brought over from Cuisine Arts. After Thanksgiving there would be only two weeks of classes until the start of the biggest party of the whole year; the three week long Festival of Lights.

The Festival of Lights honored both age old spiritual traditions from around the world and the coming together of humanity as One People. Christmas, Hanukkah, Kwanzaa, Winter Solstice, and New Years were all celebrated as everyone shared the foods, the ceremonies, and the dances of the different cultures. (If a pod mate suggested adding another tradition it would be done with that student's help.) After the older traditions, the newer traditions were honored; the telling of the First Day Story, the reading of the Peace Poem, the Oneness Dance, and the powerful Light Gathering/Light Sending Meditation.

There were also special exhibits of the residents' arts and crafts to visit in the Art Pod galleries, ongoing plays and skits put on by the Actors' Pod, sewing and quilting demonstrations and also fashion shows over at Fiber Arts, and energy balancing sessions and massages at the Healing Pod. Or one could leave the quad and head for an old-fashioned carnival or miniature golf or to see a sporting event or to hear music or whatever. Parents came from everywhere to share this happy time with their children.

Before all the excitement began, Jeori Kellog had things he wanted to get done. He sat in the window seat of his room with a sketch book balanced on his lap, a pencil in his right hand, and a ruler by his side. He planned to have his beginning sketch of the shapes of San Francisco completed by tomorrow so that next week he could begin painting the scene in acrylics. But instead of drawing the boy was staring out at the pouring rain. Wind moaned through the quad, and rain pelted his window in sheets.

To have the first big storm of the season come right before Thanksgiving was not good—not good at all. Where could they put all the relatives who would be coming in to spend the holiday? For the fourteens' Coming of Age Celebration in September they'd set up tables and extra seating along with the portable dance floor in the center of the quad, so there was plenty of room for visitors. But they couldn't do that with weather like this. Even if the sky cleared this minute, the grass and the paths would still be full of puddles on Thanksgiving Day.

Jeori sighed and grabbed his ruler to shape the pyramid he remembered. He drew the first line and then the second. He felt something change outside, his eyes drawn again to the window and then down into to center of the quad. Figures wearing yellow hooded rain slickers and backpacks had begun appearing out of thin air around the edges of the courtyard. Finally they numbered ten.

Each figure took up a position in front of one of the tall lamp posts that skirted the open space. Four feet below the tops of the posts, strong brackets held out the large globes used for night-lighting the quad.

Jeori felt a short tingle of energy as the workers began slowly rising into the air. Their backpacks were propelling them!

There was a knock on the door. "Jeori, can I come in?"

"Sure, Kayla...maybe you can tell me what's going on."

The girl joined Jeori at the window. "It's a new invention they're trying out," she replied, running a hand through her curly hair." I think it's called an air blanket or something."

"Oh, yeah...I remember now. My father told me all about this, Kayla. That air blanket thing started in my dad's physics pod in Chicago. It's a new app of force-field technology. Two twelve-year-old kids came up with the idea and brought it to one of the grown-ups. And together the three of them created the blanket."

"Right," Kayla agreed. "And that's what's so great about the pods, isn't it? You can be a child, and grownups will still take your ideas seriously." Jeori nodded.

The two ten-year-olds watched as the workers reached the very tops of the posts and began attaching the small square metal boxes they had each carried up. As soon as the workers were safely on the ground, there was a pulse of energy so strong that it vibrated the window and made the short hairs on the back of Jeori's neck stand up. Lines of blue light suddenly shot between the posts in all directions forming a web...and disappeared. The rain was now hitting an invisible shield and dissolving as it did.

"Let's go!" Kayla exclaimed. All else was forgotten as the two friends rushed downstairs, out the large double doors, and into the center of the quad. They

2065

were among the first to arrive, but soon the space was filled with people of all ages. Everyone looked up. No rain fell.

Grandma Theresa joined the growing crowd. "Quad mates," she said in a loud voice, "I'm told that the next step will be drying the grounds of excess moisture. Anyone who doesn't wish to get soaked, please leave now."

Getting soaked sounded like a *really* good idea to Kayla and Jeori, so they stayed put. So did nearly everyone else—including Grandma Theresa, who had the biggest smile ever on her wrinkled face.

Heat hit the air, and moisture began rising from the ground as steam. Soon it was so steamy that it was getting hard to see, and yes, everyone was getting soaked to the bone. Someone started a wild dance. Soon everyone was dancing. But in a few minutes the heat became too much. Clothes dried and the dancers, including Jeori and Kayla, headed back inside to return to whatever it was that they had been doing.

~ Chapter 10 ~

Years later Jeori would still remember fondly his first year with Art Pod and most especially the three weeks of the Festival of Lights. His mind would flash on the exotic foods from different cultures he'd tried for the very first time, the bright splashes of color, the music, the dancing, the hugs, and the laughter...and the look of pride on his mom's and dad's faces as he shared with them the drawings, paintings, and crafts he'd created in his first few months as a member of the Artists' Guild.

He'd remember his parents' reactions as he proudly showed them the first bowl he'd ever thrown on the solar powered potters' wheel. He was excited because his bowl hadn't collapsed on the wheel like most of the other kids' first tries. The bright red bowl *was* a bit lopsided. But Mom had said, turning it carefully in her hands, that it was the most beautiful bowl she'd ever seen.

For several years after, Jeori would still occasionally see that red bowl being used in the cafeteria. It was just the right size to serve custard or cereal or fruit. The more perfectly formed dishware created by the older apprentices and adults would either be used for their quad or given to the neighboring quads or put into the exchange where it could end up anywhere in the world.

~ ~ ~

February 5, 2065, was Jeori's first Lunar New Years celebration. He and his pod mates ate dim sum, watched a traditional parade, and a show by visiting Chinese acrobats. But the best part of all, the big finish, was the laser "fireworks" display.

Valentine's Day came and went. Jeori had little memory of it later except dressing up in a suit and tie from The Closet, dancing (mostly with Kayla) to music that was too loud, and wishing that Cyndi (who sometimes worked the kitchen and served food in the cafeteria) would show up. She never did.

Blossoming cherry trees had marked the coming of spring to the quad. As the weather grew warmer, the Tangerines took their turn helping out at Green Gardens. The older Jeori would smile as he remembered those three days of hard work, mud, and laughter.

The twenty students were given their own plot of land to tend. They cleared the weeds and took turns tilling the soil with a small solar powered cultivator. (Now that was fun!) After raking it smooth, they carefully laid out vegetable seeds in neat rows, finally sprinkling a bit of dirt on top of each seed. Then they watered their patch of earth...somehow getting as much water on themselves and each other as on their new garden.

At night they slept in tents under the starry skies staying awake late and giggling in their sleeping bags. On the Tangerine's final day, they visited the nearby farm where they petted the sheep, scattered feed for the chickens, gathered eggs, and got to try their hands at milking the contented cows. It all was such a great adventure!

And then came summertime with horseback riding lessons and ice cream and swimming in a nearby lake and painting out of doors. Jeori was getting better at throwing pots, too, and he had taken to slipping into the ceramics studio to practice on the potter's wheel whenever he had extra time.

As a young man Jeori would return to these bright memories whenever he wanted a bit more joy, a bit more energy for his various projects. So much had happened since.

Jeori could not have suspected in that first magical year that his second year in Art Pod would bring not only an unlikely friendship, but that he would be involved in a mistake which would lead into a dark and dangerous place with threads spreading out all over the world.

~ Chapter 11 ~

August 20, 2065

As sunshine hit his face, the eleven-year-old opened his blue eyes. "I joined Art Pod one year ago today," Jeori said to himself. "I can hardly believe it's been that long." He jumped out of bed, reached into his small closet, and grabbed out the white jeans and the knee-length purple smock that he had been saving for today. He pulled them on.

So today it's the color purple, Jeori thought as he buttoned the loose artist's smock. He chuckled. The ancient, tattered book with that name was Kayla's favorite. *I give her ten seconds.*

There was a rap on the door. It opened and a head, wild with red curls, popped through. "So are you reading or painting?"

"Painting. I finished glazing my last blue tile yesterday so today it's ...."

"Purple!" she finished.

"And I wish you'd stay out of my head, Kayla. It's too early for your tricks."

"Make me, Jeori!" Kayla stuck out her tongue as she entered her friend's dorm room. "Really Jeori, blocking your thoughts isn't that hard. And it's my job to give you practice while you're learning to path better. Did you hear the news about Kadrun?"

"No. What about Mr. Black?"

"He decided to leave our pod, actually. He said being an artist was boring."

The boy shook his head. "I had the feeling that might happen. I like his art...mostly just because it's *so* different, but he never really seemed to enjoy *doing*

~ 50 ~

it. And that's the thing, right? And he always seemed *so* alone...which is hard to be in a pod, isn't it?"

Jeori flashed on his first trip to the Artists' Guild nearly two years before, while he was still trying to decide where he would go next to live and study. Most kids left their birth homes when they were ten and some even younger. Mom and Dad had begun taking him to visit lots of different quads and the pods within quads on the day after his ninth birthday.

Traveling by Air Tram so exciting! And once they reached a destination there was much to explore. There were so many different ways of living from one group to the next, and so many subject areas to choose from. But as Jeori had stepped through the big double doors at the entrance to the Western Division Artists' Guild and looked up at the huge abstract painting by the fireplace, he had known. It was not the natural sciences, not healing sciences, not math, not literature, not cooking arts—or fiber arts or gardening or any of the other myriad subjects that he wanted to explore first. It was art.

As Jeori had strolled through the gallery rooms displaying the students' drawings and paintings and sculptures on that very first day, he had noticed Kadrun's art at once. It was hard to miss. If the assignment was to use shades of red, Kad's offering was black with a small red square at one corner. If the assignment was to use orange, there was another black painting with a single orange tear drop...and so on. And it was on Jeori's first day in residence, while he was still trying to find his way around, that fourteen-year-old Kad, wearing his usual black on black, had almost run the younger boy down in the hall. *Not paying attention,* Jeori thought...*lost in his little black cloud.*

"Well," said Kayla, "yesterday Kad took his little black cloud over to the Actors' Guild. Maybe he'll like being in front of an audience better. I bet he'll choose to play some of those creepy characters from the past...Count Dracula or something. That would be funny. So...are you coming down to breakfast?"

"In a minute," Jeori sighed. The door closed again. Kayla was fully telepathic, probably from the moment she was born. She was really quiet about her talent last year, but lately she had started teasing her best friend constantly with what she could do. It was just too easy for Kayla to read what was in his mind, even through the wall between their rooms. A thought struck. *Could Kad be telepathic, too? Could he just be shielding so well that nobody knew it?* To hear what people thought of you at every moment might not be so easy, especially if you had something in your past you were trying to hide.

Oops, he was late again! Jeori ran a hand through his hair and headed for the bathroom at the end of the hall. He brushed past several kids going in the opposite direction and pushed through the swinging door. The boy reached into his cubby, chose the new purple tube of toothpaste from among the rainbow of choices, and dabbed some grape flavored gel onto his short handled brush. He put it in his mouth and let go. As the brush moved around to brush each tooth he peed, washed his hands, combed his long hair and tied it back, and finally removed the brush from his mouth just as it stopped vibrating. He looked at the lavender color swirling down the drain a moment, rinsed, replaced the brush in his cubby, and hurried out.

~ Chapter 12 ~

The noise level was high when Jeori entered the cafeteria. His color study group, called Rainbow Chakras, almost always had breakfast together in one section of the massive room. Yesterday Jeori had said goodbye to his friends from Blue. He quickly located the purple section from the purple tablecloth and purple lights glittering overhead and rushed to fill the only empty seat. Half of the faces surrounding him were new. Jeori liked the fact that students were allowed to complete most of their lessons and projects at their own pace in the pod. This meant that you were always making new friends as you switched into a new level. And no one thought you were a loser if you took longer to do something than someone else. Some really great art was completed within a day and some took months. And that was all okay.

Just then Cyndi, Jeori's favorite intern from Cuisine Arts, entered the dining room from the kitchen and headed for his table. Today Cyndi was wearing a long purple velvet robe tied with a golden rope. On her head was a gold filigree crown set with purple "gems." Her shoulder-length black hair was tied back with a purple satin ribbon, but a few curls had crept out and surrounded her heart-shaped face. Like the other costumes that the servers wore each week, this was a new creation on loan from Fiber Arts which was right next door. No doubt this costume would be featured in an upcoming play put on by the Actors' Guild.

Poor Cyndi! She was doing her best to walk toward them in the slow regal manner of a queen. But her crown had started falling to one side, and she was having trouble keeping the loaded breakfast tray from falling as well.

Jeori was up in a flash! He grabbed the tray and carefully set it down at his table.

"Thank you, kind knight!" Cyndi flashed him a dimpled smile before carefully rebalancing the crown on her head and turning back towards the kitchen.

Jeori blushed wildly. He looked around. Everyone at the table was staring at him. Several raised their eyebrows. One boy even blew a kiss. Ouch!

No secrets in this group, he thought. Half of the kids at the table nodded knowingly as he they heard his thought.

Names were exchanged with the students Jeori hadn't met, and the bowl of plain yogurt was passed around. As Jeori reached out for the purple bowl of dark cherries in front of him, the bowl took off sliding away down the length of the table. Bother! He grabbed for it, but it was moving way too fast. The small girl, Emily, whom he had just met and who was maybe all of eight, was sitting at the opposite end of the table staring intently at the bowl as it moved along the purple table cloth, swerved around a plate piled high with toast, and came to a full stop directly in front of her. Emily was ready with spoon in hand. She scooped some cherries into her dish, looked up, and gave the startled newcomer an impish grin.

"She always shows off when somebody new joins us," explained the boy to Jeori's right. "What she's doing is called *telekinesis*—moving stuff with the mind. Are you duly impressed?"

"Sort of," Jeori answered, though in reality he was very impressed. He'd never seen anything like it.

Quick and before it took off as well, he grabbed

tightly to the bowl of purple moon berries sitting in front of him and swirled some into his yogurt. He watched carefully as the color of his mixture changed from soft lavender to a deep, rich purple. Yes, he would try to recreate this very color today as soon as he got to the studio. The cherries had returned also. Jeori sighed and took some. He took two pieces of the slightly burnt toast and slathered them with butter and blackberry jelly. He popped them into his mouth one after the other, all the while trying to keep up with the conversations going on around him.

~ ~ ~

As Jeori Kellogg stepped through the door of the Purple Room for the very first time, he was greeted by a long purple beaded curtain in front of his face. He pushed through the curtain and looked around. The students he had met at breakfast were already getting settled in different parts of the large room or making their way through to the connected ceramics studio. *The interns who decorated this room sure went all out,* the boy thought as he briefly checked out his new color study area. The hanging lights overhead had metal shades of purple. Curtains framing the six windows were decorated with painted purple pansies. Purple paper flowers in purple ceramic boxes lined the windowsills, and a bunch of purple grapes made out of Paper Mache hung from the ceiling. A large abstract painting in shades of purple, magenta, and lavender adorned the largest wall. *Maybe someday I'll help decorate one of the color rooms.* He took a seat at the first table which was finger painting.

No matter what Chakra color you were working in, finger painting was always Station 1. By starting with finger paints the students would receive what the teachers called "a feeling for the color." Jeori noticed the red, blue, and white finger paints in front of him now. How many different shades of purple, lavender and violet could he create with just those three colors? That was the challenge. He stuck two fingers in the red and made a smear on the paper in front of him, then did the same with blue, mixing the blue into the edge of the red. Yes! He was getting a "feeling" for the color all right...and the feeling was...*gooey!*

Jeori liked that the teachers seldom told you what you *had* to make. Being an artist was all about learning the techniques for each medium and then using your imagination to create what you wanted. Students were also encouraged to create new techniques. Because Jeori had already made his way through the red, orange, yellow, green, and blue rooms, the eleven-year-old was getting comfortable with the techniques taught at each station.

No matter which color group he was working in, Jeori always completed his experiments with Station 1 quickly. After all there was only so much you could do with finger paints. Next was Station 2—watercolor. For this station the watercolor teacher or one of the upper level interns would come around to demonstrate different techniques to the students and be available to answer questions as they came up.

After taking as long as you wanted and completing as many watercolor paintings as you wished in your color range, you would move to Station 3—acrylic painting. A different teacher or intern came around to help with this station, too. The final station, Station 4, was in the next connected room and was Jeori's absolute favorite—ceramics. Jeori loved that there were so many choices when you worked in clay. There was slab technique, hand sculpting and, what Jeori found the most exciting of all, throwing pots in all different shapes on the solar-powered potters' wheel. And there were the different glazing techniques to learn and the different choices of glazes.

After a year of making his way through Chakra Colors, Jeori felt as if he was really getting the hang of using the potters' wheel. He was already planning his first project for when he reached the ceramics section this time. He would create his very first dinner plate ever! Plates were difficult to get even, so that they looked balanced and weren't too thick, but Jeori felt certain he was finally ready for the challenge. And after blue, purple was Jeori's next favorite color. Yes, this was going to be fun!

~ Chapter 13 ~

Cleo's Diary

September 18, 2065

I'm home! I can't believe that time flies by so fast. I remember how the last Festival of Lights came and went in a blur. I'd hoped to see Kadrun at the New Year's Eve costume party and dance, but he never showed. Come to think of it I don't think I saw him once during that whole three week vacation period. Then it seemed with all the studio work to get done and prep for my trip, I turned around and it was time to leave for China.

Stephan Zuniga was...um...dreamy to teleport with! But of course all I remember is the feeling of his arms around me and the roughness of his wool coat. Then he said in his deep, beautiful voice "Are you ready, Cleo?" I nodded against his chest, and there was that odd floaty feeling, and then we were there. Nothing to it, really!

I'm sure that I'll be able to travel out further on my own now. Part of doing anything new is first knowing that its possible, then having someone show you how, and then trying it out a few times to get comfortable with it.

Oh, dear diary, China was really exciting and really, really different. In the beginning I was especially nervous because I didn't know anyone except the two girls who were supposed to show me around. Beijing pod is huge! And all the halls look pretty much the same, too, so it's easy to get lost.

Everybody was nice to me, but I found out first thing that I needed to pay close attention in classes and to be on time no matter what. The professors there are so serious.

They don't smile at all while they're teaching. And you are not allowed to take projects at your own pace the way we do here. Even when I could get from one place to another on my own and I began to make more friends, I worried constantly that I wouldn't be able to please my teachers or finish my assignments on time. The students there don't seem to mind because it is what they're used to. And I got used to the discipline after awhile, too.

I was nervous about presenting the talk about my painting technique, but both the younger students and the older people of Beijing Art Pod were really curious and even anxious to try out my method, so that part went fine.

I learned some beginning Chinese brush technique, but it takes years to really master that style of painting. I would practice one brush stroke over and over and over trying to get it right while my teacher looked over my shoulder saying "Chongfu! Chongfu! Chongfu!" "Chongfu" means "repeat." Boy! Did that make me nervous!

I met some ten and eleven-year-olds who were already doing nice well-balanced landscapes in the Chinese way. But I didn't feel too bad because it was all new to me. I also learned a lot just from studying the students' gallery art in my spare moments. And at night and on weekends I got to know many kids my own age. I must say that for students who work so hard during the day, they sure know how to play the rest of the time!

Oh—a knock on the door...................

That was Mage, checking in. She told me she had fun with Li Ha, but she sure is happy I'm home. And so am I! I can relax now. I have loads of memories and lots of vids to help me remember China.

I was asked to give a talk to the whole pod about my experiences in a couple of weeks. I'll show the vids, too. Before I went to China I would have worried about giving a talk in front of all the kids and the adults at once, but now it *seems easy. That's because I'm in my own pod again. And we're all family.*

~ Chapter 14 ~

Jeori's Journal

Today in Past Class we got an assignment. We have two weeks to do it, but it looks easy. We have to write our own pasts down starting with how our parents met. I'm going to try it now right here. Then I'll compute it up cleaner.

Jeori's Story (I like that! Ha-ha!)
*So my mom and dad might never have met up except for something that could have been a disaster! They lived on different sides of Amerada. My mom was already an architect in Western Division Community Planning. (That's in the next quad over—very close!) But my dad was still finishing school in the Mid-western Division Physics Pod. (That's where he is now.) Anyway, that day Melody—that's my mom—her mom wanted her to be a singer but she didn't want to—was out in the middle of a big open space looking at where to put a new building she was helping to design. Suddenly a tall man appeared out of nowhere knocking her down to the ground! Raphael—that's my dad—he's named after an angel—had teleported almost on top of her! I guess that's the danger with teleporting, but I don't care. **I really don't!!** He was on vacation.*

After that crazy way of meeting, they started visiting each other's pods and going to plays and museums and sports events together. And they got that warm feeling that means love. So they decided to take the courses and get licensed to be parents. Then they would be given a nice house with furniture and dishes and stuff for the time they took to raise me.

You know what happened next? Me happened! If you could see me hold up my shirt right now you would see something. No belly button! That's fine with me because there is one less place to keep clean. See, Mom was finishing a big project so she didn't want to get sick sometimes and fat by being pregnant. So after they passed their tests to be parents, I was made in a vat of goo.

First they put some of Dad's sperm and a couple of Mom's eggs (I guess a couple?) in a bowl and stirred slowly. Then they scoped to see what would happen next. And the two parts came together, and that was the tiny beginning of ME! Then the bowl of me was poured (I'm not certain about this part) out into a bigger vat of gooey stuff and awhile later there I was—a beautiful baby boy! (I figured most of this out myself in case you can't tell.) Mom was right there to hold me first after I was lifted out, after I started breathing and the goo was cleaned up. And then Dad held me in his arms. Mom had to take some shots for awhile so she could give me her own milk 'cause everybody knows that's better for the baby.

Then they took me to our new family home. They stayed very close loving me and holding me and playing with me for the first year of my life. Sometimes one would go away for a little while to take a walk alone or meditate, but mostly they were with me like the vids say is good. I don't remember this part now very well, but I do remember the love feeling. I still carry it right here in my heart.

Then when I was about two years old, I started going to our community playhouse in the mornings to play with the other kids who lived near us. Either Mom or Dad would come too, at first. And then there were just us kids and Mz. Tierny and sometimes two teens, a boy and his twin sister, who came in to play with us and hand out treats. And there were lots and lots of toys, building blocks and paints and paper and clay and puzzles and costumes and vids and sometimes dogs or cats were brought in to play with us, too. There was an outside play area with a play structure. Why am I telling you all this? It's like any other playhouse anywhere. (Remember to delete this part.) We went home at 1. Then it was lunch and nap. (This part is stupid. EVERY kid gets lunch and naptime. Take this out, too.)

So it went like this and it was fun. When I got older I watched lots of learning vids with Mom and Dad. I practiced writing and drawing pictures. Mom put the teaching tabs in my ears at night so I could learn stuff in my sleep, too. That way I learned to read and to know all about numbers and geography and stuff. I also learned beginning Spanish in my sleep. I would rush to the breakfast table yelling "Comer con gusto!"

Sometimes I would walk next door to Mr. Grant's house to hear a story. He was old then and he is older now. He still has lots of the books his father read to him when he was a child. And he told me stories about what it was like growing up before everything changed. Mr. Grant has lived in that very same house since he was a tiny baby. Mr. Grant is smart! He can build anything out of wood—toys and doorknobs and chairs and shelves—whatever the pods need, and he trades them so he can have plenty to eat and still live alone which is how he likes it.

One day my folks told me that someday I would be big enough to go to a real pod to live and learn and that I would choose it myself. Now that was exciting to think about! So here I am in Art Pod, just where I wanted to be most of all. I've made my way through all the Chakra Colors to purple. We do all kinds of media in one color group and then move to the next. I really like ceramics.

I have a best friend whose name is Kayla. She's great at pathing. I want to learn how to be telepathic, too...how to hear people's thoughts just like she does.

2065

I see Mom sometimes on weekends since she lives close and Dad sometimes, too, but not so often. Thinking about the quantum field keeps him really busy.

Oh, one more thing. (Put this in earlier?) Maggie, the neighbor kid who hit me sometimes and bit my arm once at the playhouse, left with her parents suddenly when I was seven and she was five. The house next to Mr. Grant was just empty except for the furniture, and then another couple moved in with their baby. I didn't mind, because Maggie was a biter. But I asked Mom. Did they move somewhere?

That's when Mom told me that some people are not comfortable being parents even after they take the classes and get the license. So I guess Maggie's mom and dad just dropped her one day at Ladybug Playhouse and didn't come back. That sounds mean. But it was probably for the best. I saw her last year when I was over there helping out on a Saturday. I'm not sure Maggie remembered me, but she was smiling and playing with the younger children. I think she finally got love. I will never have a child if I can't love them. And that's a promise.

~ Chapter 15 ~

Jeori's Journal

Life is a river, but we get to choose the boat. That's what the teachers say anyway. What they mean is that we can make our experience in this world easy and fun or difficult and complicated depending on how we put ourselves into it. That's not to say the river always runs smoothly. Sometimes we hit a challenging section with rapids, and if we chose an old heavy clunker boat we might not tip over, but we won't have fun either. If our boat is a poorly constructed raft we will fall off the side and get swept away. But a light, well constructed boat is the thing—a boat that handles well and is adaptable to any changes in the river that we might encounter. And we can always change our course.

On Monday I decided to trade in my tired old worrying clunker for one of those sleek new boats. I gave up worrying about not being as good as Kayla with her telepathy, or little Em who moves stuff with her thoughts all the time. I decided to be me.

I'm going to be an artist and a writer and I'm going to illustrate my own books and vids. And I'm going off grounds to practice teleportation when no one else is around. Usually you have to be older. There's classes and stuff. But I really, really, REALLY want to learn how to disappear from one place and show up in another. SO I WILL!!

My boat is fast and bright blue with a white stripe. No one will even see me coming!

Jeori put away his journal and turned off the light by his bed.

Dear Journal,

I know I said it was okay that I couldn't path or do some things as well as my friends...especially Kayla. I have my sleek little boat and all that. That was then. What happened was that three weeks ago I finally started Beginning Telepathy class. I thought I'd do okay...especially since I can hear my angel. I'd learn how to hear people's thoughts, too...easy with training, right? WRONG! Lots of kids who started with me tested out in the first week and more in the second. And now there are only six of us left. SIX!! To make it worse, Dharma says that next week we may have ten newbies joining us. I have been trying SO hard. All of us have. I'm getting pretty good at feeling emotions when we team up, but that's not much proof, 'cause we're all feeling pretty much the same—upset and stupid...stupid...STUPID.

Hi journal,

Well, today was sure different. Our teacher, Dharma, said he was sorry. He said he had forgotten how it felt to be a kid and not be able to get something right away—especially when lots of your friends did. He said he was not good at pathing at first either. So he said we would only play from now on. No more testing. No more trying hard to do anything. And it would just be the six of us for as long as we wanted to keep getting together.

None of us could figure what he meant at first about playing. But then he said he wanted us to just pretend what each other was thinking. He said please be outrageous... please make up crazy things, the crazier the better!! So we spent the next hour laughing!

I said Martin was thinking about how much he wanted to lick a tasty frog. Ben said Khan was thinking about his last great fart. And Khan said Ben was planning to teleport to Mars which was stupid because he wouldn't be able to breathe there.   Marlie said I was thinking about kissing Annabel. I said I was not! (Weird thing was yesterday I did see Annabel kissing some older guy in the hall.) Time went by so fast. Nobody checked to see if we got anything right, but we sure had fun! And I think I maybe got a hit of what Lily Ann was really thinking one time. But I didn't say,' cause those are the new rules. My sleek little boat is skimming right along again!

~ Chapter 16 ~

Cleopatra Murphy's fifteenth birthday on September 22, 2065 should have been the happiest of days. She was back from China, in her own pod again with her friends and with loads of memories as well as a new beginning skill in Chinese brush painting. She'd gotten the advanced computer gaming class she'd chosen as an elective this time, and her other classes and studios were good. She looked forward to vid conferencing with her parents tonight when they would wish their daughter a very happy birthday. All should have been perfect.

But at 3:45 in the afternoon as she was making her way to the studio to work on her new oil painting, Cleo overheard someone mention Kadrun Connelly. She hadn't run into Kad since she'd been back, but she'd been busy—and it had only been six days since her return so she had thought nothing of it. She stopped to listen in.

"Mr. Black left our pod to be an *actor*," Katalina was saying to Gavrielle in what Cleo thought was a snide voice.

"He sure was different," was her friend's more neutral reply.

Cleo walked on shaking her head. Maybe Mage would know more. Why hadn't her best friend said anything? Cleo didn't know why she should care. She and Kad had only worked together for two class periods in Games Creation, and he had called her an elf. That was the sum total of their "relationship." She took a deep breath. *Get a hold of yourself, birthday girl,* she thought.

Cleo Murphy rearranged her blue artist's smock, pushed through the swinging studio doors, and moved towards her easel and the painting she'd begun two days before. She had felt so happy with how this painting was coming along. But now as her gaze landed on what she had done, it felt entirely wrong.

Cleo frowned at the sunny yellow sky she had painted in first. Into that palest shade of yellow she had concentrated the feeling of hope. Into the brighter yellow hue with an undertone of orange, she had added the excitement of something wonderful waiting just around the corner. She had focused the feeling of happiness at new beginnings into the green that formed the rounded hillsides. The darker green color of the fir trees with their low hanging branches was all about mystery and magic. And because of the contrast in color and texture, it was to those fir trees that your eyes were naturally drawn.

Until this very moment Cleo hadn't realized what her painting was saying. But suddenly it was obvious. And with one overheard conversation everything had changed. The mystery man she hoped to touch with her sunshine was gone. And the green happiness that she had imagined connecting them was gone, too. Kad had only moved across the quad. But because the two pods rarely got together for activities it seemed to Cleo that Kadrun Connelly might as well be on the moon.

The fifteen-year-old sighed as she looked down at her tubes of paint. Her painting would change into something entirely different now. She grabbed the tube of ultramarine blue and squeezed some out onto her pallet. Next she added a bit of cadmium red, a large blob of titanium white, and some Paynes gray.

Cleo slowly began to mix first a shade of lavender-blue and then one of gray-blue. Into the first she concentrated sudden unwanted change and into the second unexpected sadness. Over the green hillside, blue shadows would form as a front of clouds rushed in to cover the sun. The mysterious trees would become less distinct now and seem further away. Soon the once bright day and the dark trees would feel the coming of rain.

Stupid tear, Cleo thought and brushed it away with the back of her hand. She picked up one of her larger brushes and began to make the changes.

~ Chapter 17 ~

October 06, 2065

Cleo Murphy shook her head. *Looks like it's me.* She pocketed her small phone and moved to the front of the cafeteria tables. She cleared her throat and looked around at the twenty younger students. "Professor Zuniga was held up, so he asked me to begin introducing today's field trip. I'm sure you're all probably curious. There's been a lot of secrecy around where we'll be going and what we'll be seeing.

"First, welcome Aardvarks to your first field activity of the school year—and maybe the most interesting! I think by now I've met nearly all of you second years. My name is Cleopatra Murphy. I was asked to be one of your chaperones today along with Mike Constantine, who is also a third level intern here at Art Pod." (Mike stood and quickly sat down again.)

"Stephan Zuniga, who teaches printmaking techniques and advanced teleportation, will be here soon. I hope you all brought your sketch pads. For those of you who....

"Noodle! Some attention up here would be good." Cleo stared at the large-boned, blond haired Igor Nudleman who was widely known as the life of any Art Pod party. (And to Igor any day was party day.) Twelve-year-old Noodle was right in the middle of telling a joke to the red-haired girl directly across from him. He looked up. The girl he had been entertaining, Kayla Landry, squeezed her eyes tight in embarrassment. Jeori Kellogg, sitting to one side of his best friend, shook his head.

"Okay," Cleo continued. "Today we will be traveling by Lavender Line Air Transit to one of the old cities." Excited whispers began. Cleo noisily cleared her throat and thought, *Quiet!* "The weather forecast says we may see the very first snowfall of the season today in...Are you ready for it?.... Cleo paused dramatically. "Denver, Colorado!"

Denver? Jeori thought. *But that's so far away!* From the looks on the faces of the other Aardvarks, no one else could believe it either.

"So before we leave for the Veet Van, please choose one of the warm hooded coats in your size from the front closet.

"What will we be doing in the mile high city, you ask? As you know, most of the cities left on Earth have been taken over by the scientists, inventors, and teckies for living space as well as for laboratories, new inventions, and manufacturing of different kinds. Today we will be visiting ...." Cleo felt a sudden change in energy. "Oh, here comes Professor Zuniga now....

"Thanks so much, Cleo," Stephan Zuniga said in his deep voice as he suddenly appeared out of thin air by the cafeteria door and walked over, looking a little wind-blown from his translocation. Cleo sat down.

"I apologize for being late. There was a bit of an early morning teleportation emergency...a bit of search and rescue. So...Denver, Colorado it is! Denver is known for having the finest, the most advanced robotics center on Earth."

Robots? The twenty Aardvarks looked around at their table mates, smiles forming and eyes wide.

"All of our robotic vacuum devices or Vac-bots —which I might add some of you have tripped over while skulking through the halls after midnight—

were developed and created at the Rocky Mountain Robotics Pod."

A quick glance passed between Noodle and his three best friends; the self-named "Night Marauders." Then Igor sat up straight and boldly looked around as if trying to spot the guilty parties.

Professor Zuniga sighed. "First we'll visit the Robot Museum to learn about the early robots—what they were designed to do, and what they could accomplish. Next we will move on to the practical robotics in use today; for example, the Laundry-bots that clean, fold, and deposit clothing into our closets during the night, the tall Rescue-bots which find people missing in the woods or on mountain tops, and the smaller Scow-bots which patrol the seas gathering surface garbage still left over from the before time. We will also explore the more exciting up and coming robot advances being developed on a nearly daily basis by the excited students and scientists of the Robotics Guild.

"As Cleo may have mentioned, we will also have the opportunity to sketch the robots we visit. So I hope you all have your sketch books and pencils with you. The sketches you do today may be used later in your art and craft projects. Those of you interested in exploring caricature, cartoon, vid art, and games creation should especially enjoy this. But regardless, I'm sure all of you will find our trip today truly fascinating. Obviously I expect you to all be on your best behavior." Stephan Zuniga scanned the tables, his eyes landing momentarily on Igor Nudleman.

Jeori smiled at Kayla and Kayla raised her eyebrows and smiled back. They were both thinking the same thing. *This is going to be the best field trip ever!*

~ Chapter 18 ~

A quick van ride brought the warmly bundled Aardvarks to the A.T. station, and in minutes they were flying through the puffy cloud-filled morning sky in their lavender colored, force field driven tram. For once there was no desire to talk as the students took in the passing scenery beneath them.

In less than an hour the Lavender Line train pulled to a stop at the Denver station. The students and their chaperones stepped off the train onto the platform. *Brrr!* It was cold! They sped down the two levels of escalators to discover their first surprise. The "person" waiting to greet them was a robot—a six foot six silicon robot with slick black hair, bright blue eyes, and translucent pink skin. It was wearing a snug green jumpsuit, soft black shoes and...oddly out of place, a man's green and black checkered necktie. It opened its mouth.

"Many Greetings, Art Pod Aardvarks. My name is Rob-Ort, and I am one of four Hospitality-bots for Rocky Mountain Robotics Guild. Robo-van Number Four is at this moment forty seconds from our current location. After the van has made a complete stop, the doors will open. Please take your seats quickly and quietly. I will accompany you. The van is programmed to automatically return to its point of origin. This it will complete in exactly five minutes, thirty seconds from departure.

"A caution: Please do not kick or in any way attempt to damage or disable any robotic device. Be aware: If harm is attempted to this or any other unit, an alarm will sound and the miscreant will be ejected from the tour and subjected to torture."

Every one of the second years gasped.

"Ha-ha. That last part was a joke," Rob-Ort said as a stiff smile came to its pale lips.

~ ~ ~

The robo-van arrived and the doors slid open. All the Aardvarks took their seats quietly, everyone still a little in shock from Rob-Ort's "joke."

A small smile came to Cleo's face as she watched the students find seats. She remembered when the identical "joke" was said to her activity group, the Turtles, during her second year trip four years ago. It had gotten the same reaction then. *The people who planned this experience sure know how to take control of a group,* she thought.

As she'd been instructed, Cleo stayed back and watched the students as they made their way through the Museum of Robot History. They saw the mock-up of what was considered the first robotic device; a steam-driven mechanical bird created in China in 350 BC, and the water clock with moveable features created in Greece in 270 BC. There was a section of old world books suggesting artificially created life forms, the first being Mary Shelley's 1818 book "Frankenstein."

The museum tour was the same as Cleo had experienced—from a copy of the 1921 Czech play, "Rossum's Universal Robots," in which the word "robot" was used for the very first time, to books mentioning robots by science fiction writer Isaac Asimov, to old photographs of the first robotics company started in 1956, and the first industrial robot, which was nicknamed "Unimate." Then there were photos and a vid of the use of robotics in manufacturing and medicine in the nineteen sixties. The students saw the first electrically controlled robot arm ever created, prosthetic legs, and realistic looking and moving hands. Next the Aardvarks saw pictures and descriptions of robotic devices used in space exploration of Mercury, Venus, Mars, and beyond. Then to top it all off there were photographs and descriptions of the common robots and robotic devices in use and the newest discoveries of the age.

Cleo stifled a chuckle as she watched the students frown and shake their heads as they came to the end of the exhibit and realized that all they had been shown were pictures of robots instead of the actual ones. Yes, it was all just as she remembered.

Next Rob-Ort led the group down a long, narrow, and rather dizzying hallway made entirely of shiny steel. At the end of the hall was a door with a lighted exit sign. Rob-Ort turned to face the group. "Thank you so much for visiting us here at the Rocky Mountain Robotics Guild. We hope you enjoyed the tour as much as we have enjoyed giving it to you." The robot paused and again flashed that eerie smile. "Good bye."

There were a few groans. "That's it?" someone asked. Without a missed beat the door behind the robot slid slowly open. "Follow me, please, one by one and line the wall. Oh, and please watch your step. We wouldn't want you to step in anything unpleasant. Ha-ha," added Rob-Ort."

A bit timidly the Aardvarks did as they had been instructed watching their feet just in case there was something on the floor. They found themselves lining a large, empty room lit only by the light coming in from the hallway. The door slid shut, and they were in complete darkness. There was hardly a sound, but Jeori felt a change in the air. Something was moving around in front of them.

Suddenly different colored spotlights splayed down from the ceiling as music began playing. In the center of the room ten couples were dancing, twirling, and gyrating to the strains of Rocket Roll. These of course were colorfully dressed robots—fairly short ones at that—close in size to the eleven and twelve-year-olds who watched in surprise. The boy robots were dressed in black suits, and the girl robots wore different colored dresses with flared skirts.

The music began to soften as the bots danced on. Now the boy robots were swinging the girl robots around. Now the boy robots were lifting the girl robots over their heads.

"We at the Rocky Mountain Robotics Guild proudly present our latest generation of Dance-bots," Rob-Ort announced from his position near the opposite wall. "You may applaud now," he prodded. The stunned audience began to clap their hands—slowly at first and then with more enthusiasm.

The music changed, and the Dance-bots moved into an upbeat tango. At another change they began a stately waltz. "Our bots know all the popular old world dances as well as the dances of our modern age. This is merely a preview. In approximately a year these fabulous creations and others like them will be used to teach dance technique in pods the world over.

"Now, how many of you would be willing to help our Dance-bots practice? How many of you would like a dance lesson today?" Rob-Ort slowly turned his head as if looking each student in the eye.

No one moved. No one answered. If it had been possible to scoot backwards the students of Art Pod would have done just that. But there was nowhere to go. They were already standing against the wall.

As if anticipating their reaction Rob-Ort said, "Come now, Aardvarks! This is perfectly safe. Remember the robots' first rule is never to hurt a human. Wouldn't you like to be able to dance beautifully at the next Festival of Lights celebration? Wouldn't you like to impress that certain special boy or girl? Well, *of course you would!*"

The Dance-bots suddenly stopped dancing and walked over, each taking a position in front of one of the children. They reached out their left hands and said in unison, "Will you kindly give me the pleasure of this dance?"

After a few awkward moments, one student then another took a robot's hand and moved out onto the dance floor. Soon each child was engaged in learning the first dance, a waltz, with their robot. "Step one-forward, two-back, step three-to the right, four-back! Very good!" the Dance-bots said.

Once Jeori got over his squeamishness at even touching a robot, he realized he was actually starting to have fun as his girl-bot moved around with him on the dance floor telling him what to do next and saying "Good job" or "What a fast learner you are" every few minutes.

With their robot partners leading, the twenty students learned the waltz, the tango, the fox trot, and the swing. Then they practiced the new world dances; the oneness dance, the Venus slide, the mango, and the tandem woogy. Finally the robots stood back as the twenty boys and girls practiced the different dance steps with each other.

All was going smoothly until twelve-year-old Matthew decided it would be a great idea to swing eleven-year-old Sophia around in the same way the robots had during their beginning demonstration. Unfortunately after ten minutes of doing the tandem woogy, Matt's hands were slick with sweat. Sophie slipped out of his grip in mid-air, and a moment later she hit the floor with a loud "Oomph." The girl stood slowly and brushed herself off.

A stiff smile came to Rob-Ort's face. "Ahem," the robot said. "That is not a dance step I recognize."

Everyone laughed...well, nearly everyone. Sophie glared at Matt, and Matt shrugged his shoulders and mouthed *Sorry*.

~ Chapter 19 ~

Rob-Ort moved his gaze dramatically around the room. "We are extremely pleased that you have enjoyed your lessons with our Dance-bots today as well as the tour of our excellent museum. This then marks the end of your tour of the Rocky Mountain Robotics Guild. This way, please."

The now familiar smile returned to Rob-Ort's face just before he turned and walked stiffly toward a second door under yet another exit sign, which had just lighted at the opposite end of the room.

This time not one of the twenty students took it for granted that this was really the end of their field trip. They followed the hospitality robot under the exit sign...and directly into the biggest and tallest room any of them had ever seen!

"Ha-ha" said Rob-Ort. "I am so amusing. I fooled you again."

The students of Art Pod barely heard Rob-Ort this time. They were far too busy looking around themselves in wonder. Robots and robotic devices of all kinds and sizes stood everywhere.

The largest robot of all, the giant copper-colored search and rescue unit, stood right at the room's center, the top of its metal head coming within twenty feet of the hundred foot ceiling. Without warning beams of red light began shooting from the robot's eyes, and the giant head started slowly swiveling back and forth as if it was searching for something. One hand moved up as if to shade its eyes. "Who am I looking for today?" it said in a loud, rumbling voice.

Several of the Aardvarks took a step backwards bumping into the ones behind them. "Students," Rob-Ort said, "do not be at all concerned by my large friend. He is merely doing what he is designed to do. Willard here may be big, but he is as gentle as a tiny kitten. Isn't that right, Willard?" A thoroughly unsettling and terribly loud "meow" echoed through the chamber. Jeori reflexively grabbed Kayla's hand.

"Ha-Ha," Rob-Ort repeated and smiled. "Art Pod Aardvarks! Before you on the floor you will notice a triple row of large squares. Every other square contains a lighted letter and number. Please pick one of these to stand in...now!" Rob-Ort looked around as the students timidly chose places. Cleo noticed that even the usually boisterous Igor Nudleman remained quiet as he chose a square.

This X-14 looks like a good number, Jeori thought. He took a place on the square marked X-14. Kayla stood next to him on Y-5.

"Now consider this!" Rob-Ort's voice echoed off the walls of the huge chamber. "Each of our robotic devices serves a different function. Your job for today, Aardvarks, is to first carefully follow the lighted path to your own robot and then to discover what your device can do.

"Remember to speak to your robot in a clear voice addressing it first by name. For example: 'Robot A-22, move to the back wall and turn around.' You must use the same tone beginning with your robots name to reverse the process. For example: 'Robot A-22, move to your starting point and stop.' Very well, students! Look at your feet and...*Go!*"

Jeori and Kayla looked at each other and then down at their feet. Instantly small circular green lights appeared on the floor marking a pathway from each square out into some other portion of the giant room. At the end of each path their robots would be waiting.

The two friends waved goodbye to each other and began to follow their own pathways. Jeori quickly discovered that the lighted paths didn't go in straight lines. Instead they wove through one another in swerving or spiral or zigzag patterns. The challenge was to pay attention so you didn't cross onto someone else's path by mistake or end up going back the way you had come and find yourself again at the starting point. Instead of the wild excitement and running around that would be tempting for a group of twenty pre-teens in a cavernous room full of robots, there was absolute quiet as the students each concentrated on reaching the end of their pathway and finding their own robot.

The excitement was building as Jeori Kellogg reached the end of his lighted path, which had led him all the way to the back of the room near one corner. He stared with disbelieving eyes at what was standing directly before him.

"No!" he breathed. But it was model X-14 all right, its name painted red on its side as proof, looking just like the squat brown Vac-bot that it was. Disappointment hit Jeori like a blow. He looked around. Everyone was reaching the end of their paths now and greeting their robots with smiles. The eleven-year-old spotted several medium-sized robots and a couple of shorter ones nearby, all humanoid and all interesting looking. He spied one that looked like a giant crab with big pinchers and another shaped like an ice cream cone with arms. His was the only cleaning model in sight. "Dang," he breathed.

"All right," Jeori said giving up on anything better, "let's see what you can do." First he ordered the unit to vacuum a dirty piece of carpet which had obviously been placed nearby for this purpose. Then he ordered the X-14 to go to the corner, extend its cleaning wand, and clean up as high as it could reach. The Vac-Bot completed this mission. The arm had reached up twelve whole feet. "Whoopee," Jeori muttered. He ordered X-14 to stay where it was with arm and wand extended.

The boy sighed. He took his sketch book and pencil from his backpack, sat down on the floor, and began to draw his bot. He formed the rounded oblong body first and then drew a smiley face on the side of it. He put freckles on the smiley face and added big teeth. He blackened a tooth. Next he drew the cleaning wand, and with a flourish added a fluttering flag at the end of the duster. He put a sun in the middle of the flag and drew some clouds floating overhead.

Jeori looked up. Had someone called his name? He looked around. Robots were slowly walking here and there responding to the commands of their "owners." Nearby Jeori noticed the ice cream model present Allie with a chocolate ice cream cone that came out of a door in its refrigerated belly. Jeori's stomach growled. Why hadn't he chosen *that* model?

There it was again. Someone *was* calling his name. It sounded like Kayla. And not only that! His best friend seemed to actually be calling in *the center of his head*. But where *was* she?

Jeori grabbed up his things and leaving his vacuum unit behind, he began to search. He walked carefully between the different students and their robots making a slow circuit which gradually led inward toward the center of the room. Jeori spotted the Laundry-bot in front of a table with a pile of laundry, and a stack that it had already neatly folded. It took one more piece from the pile, folded it, and added it to the pile. Jeori noted that the student controlling it was having only slightly more fun than he'd had with his vacuuming model.

Jeori searched high and low—but no Kayla. She seemed to have disappeared. Near the center of the room he finally discovered a clue. Standing all by itself was a blue clad hospitality robot with Y5 emblazoned on its chest. But if that was Kayla's bot, where was she?

Jeori turned and nearly tripped over the gigantic feet of the biggest, most magnificent robot in the place, the eighty-foot-tall search and rescue model. He backed up and right into—Igor Nudleman. "Uh, sorry," he said and turned around. "Noodle...is that... is that the robot you got?" he asked, suddenly envious. Jeori noticed a large doll lying on the floor a few feet away.

"Well, you see...I didn't mean it," the boy said with a nervous quaver in his voice. Jeori noticed that Noodle's normally ruddy face was pale and slick with sweat. "See, I heard her thinking about how really great it would be to be saved by a...."

"No...no, you didn't!" Jeori bellowed. "Kayla's up there?" The older boy nodded meekly. "Noodle, how could you?" Jeori looked up, but he was too close to the giant robot to see anything.

"I've been trying to get him to put her down. I really have! But he won't listen to me or I'm not saying the right words or using the right voice...or...or... something...I don't know," he whined.

Jeori backed up until he could just make out Kayla's feet dangling from the robot's open hand. "Kayla! Kayla! It's me, Jeori," he called. Are you okay?"

"I'm okay," she replied in a voice Jeori could hardly hear, what with the distance and the surrounding noise. "Just get me down."

"Noodle, listen to me closely," Jeori said with an edge of panic in his voice. "I'll go get help. Don't do anything. Don't say anything. Just stay put. I'll be right back."

Jeori moved off quickly, weaving through his friends and their robots, searching frantically for Mr. Zuniga or either of the two interns. He ran into Cleopatra Murphy first. Stumbling over his words Jeori told her what had happened. They rushed off to find Professor Zuniga. Within a couple of minutes the three of them had joined Igor Nudleman, and all four were staring up at the Rescue-bot's outstretched hand with Kayla still sitting on it, her legs kicking idly through the open fingers.

Moments later a woman from the control room arrived. She ordered the robot to "carefully lower the victim you have saved to the ground." The robot immediately did as it was instructed. Kayla stepped out happy and unhurt, Jeori hugged Kayla in relief, and the shaken Igor Nudleman was led to a place where he could lie down until he felt better.

After nearly an hour of drawing pictures of the different kinds of robots and eating a light lunch of turkey sandwiches, fruit salads, and nut bars laid out by newly designed Serving-bots in the Robotics Pod cafeteria (both of which Noodle missed because he was asleep) the students of Art Pod were again on Air Transit traveling home. Luckily someone had remembered Igor Nudleman at the last minute. He sat quietly now...nibbling on a nut bar and staring out the window.

2065

Jeori glanced over at Kayla who was entertaining some of her girlfriends with the story of her "rescue." He shook his head. *Kayla was the one stuck way up high sitting in a robot's hand—and the only person who wasn't a bit worried. My best friend is really brave.* Jeori smiled and closed his eyes as the air tram flew toward home.

~ Chapter 20 ~

Jeori's Journal

October 14, 2065

So yesterday a bunch of us...me, Ansel, Jake, Michiko and Allie...decided to try dem popping on our own. We've been taking Lance's Interdimensional Travel class for a whole month. So...time to practice, right? Only one thing we forgot. There's always one thing which seems like nothing at all...but ends up being huge.

We met at the bench in West Quad at 3. We walked slowly...looking casual and trying to keep our thoughts clear instead of shouting our excitement. We went between the Actors' Pod and Fiber Arts into the meadow and to a secret place we'd discovered under the cover of the branches and leaves of a big shade tree. A few yellow leaves had already fallen from the tree, but there were still enough left to make a real good hiding place.

We cleared our spaces and lay down giggling. We wished each other a good journey. Then we started the pattern just like Lance showed us.

I pictured the white screen in my mind. I put my hand through it. I felt the water running down the rock face of my starting place which is a cave, turned toward the tunnel entrance, and walked out into the light. I was on Earth Two standing right beside the white two-story farmhouse. The day was clear and sunny. Children were running and playing down the curved lawn that leads to the bright little stream I remembered splashing in during my last trip. I looked around. I could feel Michiko for a moment, maybe over in the cornfield across the stream, but not the others.

(It's a big planet and we all have our own starting places.) Then she was gone.

Time for me to go, too! I imagined floating in the thick feeling water of the water planet in whatever dimension it is...sorry, I can't remember. And I was there! I just looked and felt and sort of smelled the water and the other creatures around me. They look sort of like slugs and are mostly the same except maybe a little difference in color...and some are bigger. But I knew that they wouldn't hurt me because I've been there before and they didn't. So I just floated around feeling their tickling energies as they talked or sent to each other or whatever it is they do. And I opened up to try to get what they were saying. Did I get it? Maybe I did get something this time. I got a feeling of some kind of gathering they were moving toward. That was all. But it was something!

I don't know how long I was there because time loses meaning. But finally I felt an urge to go back. When I returned to Earth Two, I was sitting on the farmhouse lawn. I walked into the cave and down the tunnel and touched the water on the rock wall again. It turned into the white screen and opened my eyes. I was the first one back.

Jake was next to open his eyes followed by Allie and then Michiko...but no Ansel. He just lay there looking stiff and cold. I gently put my jacket over him so I wouldn't wake him suddenly. We're not supposed to touch someone while they're in trance. They could get stuck somewhere? I'm not sure why. Anyway we waited and waited. It was getting colder. Sunset was coming on, and then the first few stars started to wink their light down through the tree branches.

We decided we had to find our teacher. Lance was the only one who knew the code word. That's what we forgot! The code word would bring us out of trance immediately, but he had blocked it away in his mind to keep it a secret... probably so no one would try what we did.

Michiko stayed with Ansel's body while the rest of us took off running. I checked the cafeteria first, ran the stairs up to my room to get another jacket, hit Lance's classroom and finally the gallery. No good!

I practically ran full force into Jake in one of the empty hallways. Jake informed me that Allie had found Lance in a darkened studio with my painting teacher, Lydia. All us boys like Lydia. She's amazing.

Well, you don't have to know what they were doing... and that's that.

Soon we were all together again under the tree. Lance had brought a beam so we could see. He whispered the code in Ansel's ear. Ansel woke up shivering and crying.

The rest of us headed to the kitchen to get a late dinner while Lance carried Ansel over to the healing pod. A whole day later and that's where he still is. Something really scary happened to Ansel out there. I guess Lance will tell us more in class tomorrow. He didn't say anything at all about what we did...yet.

~ Chapter 21 ~

Tuesday morning came and went quite normally in Art Pod. Jeori worked up a design for his purple plate on a piece of paper. Then he began painting the first layer of glaze on his dinner-sized plate so it could go in the kiln to get fired. Michiko was in his class. They shared a look.

The eleven-year-old couldn't get his mind off the events of the weekend. Could Ansel have died if they hadn't found Lance to bring him out? Just how dangerous was dem popping anyway? This afternoon hopefully they would learn more. Maybe Lance would come down on them. Who knew?

Lunch was over and swimming class flew by. Jeori took a deep, cleansing breath as he walked through the door into Interdimensional Travel. Lance did not look up from his desk. Jeori looked around for his fellow dem poppers. They were all there—everyone except Ansel.

Their teacher looked up. He cleared his throat. "Today we have a story of the weekend misadventures of a rag tag bunch of dem poppers." There were questioning glances around the room. Four of the students looked down at their desk tops. "How many of you have heard the term dem popping?" Someone giggled. Every student but one slowly raised their hands.

"Ah...this is thought to be a secret term whispered in the cafeteria. Is that right?" Several nodded. "Do any of you know which bright and adventurous student first made up this term nearly fifteen whole years ago?" Everyone shook their heads. "Don't you, really?" Lance glanced around the room. There was a look in his eye. "Give me this scoundrel's name at once!"

Jeori's hand flew up in spite of himself. "Lance Kartoofle!" he blurted.

"Indeed." Nervous laughter broke the suspense of the moment before. "And can any one of you guess exactly why I have asked you to practice interdimensional travel in class rather than off hiding under a tree, perhaps?" There were four audible groans. "I plan to say this once so you will really hear it." Then without words he blasted the answer into each of their minds. *Because I did it, and I almost didn't come back!*

Jeori couldn't decide whether he felt more afraid or more guilty or more excited. He had heard Lance's thought loud and clear—every burning word of it!

~ Chapter 22 ~

Jeori's Journal

Ansel is coming home. All of us who were there are really curious about what happened, but we are really relieved, too. I bet we'll find out more in class tomorrow. Good night, journal.

In Thursday morning's ceramics class, Jeori got to play the part of the grieving artist. Moments before the boy had so very carefully placed his newly designed plate on the shelf to await its final firing. The plate was flawlessly formed, and he simply loved the pattern he had come up with this time. The final layer of glaze would be perfect!

Meanwhile Matt was goofing around with Sophie as usual. Matt grabbed for Sophie's braid. Sophie pulled away, and as she did she accidentally bumped the drying shelf. Jeori's newest creation went flying, and not enabled with anti-grav, the plate on which he had spent so much time crashed to the floor. It broke into a bunch of noisy pieces.

Without a word Matt and Sophie picked up the broken shards and placed them into the discard basket. Almost nothing was wasted in Art Pod. What was left of Jeori's plate might one day be found in a mosaic stepping stone or a table top or a mural. The guilty parties apologized smiling. Did that make anything better?

Jeori's face was red as he slammed a new lump of clay down on the work table as hard as he possibly could. Before he even had the gray lump flattened out, the tone chimed signaling the end of ceramics class until next week.

In the cafeteria Jeori was still mad. Lunch was tasteless. He jumped in the pool and swam his laps in his fastest time ever. It helped for him to push himself in the water. It helped to be sore. And the hot shower... that helped, too. Before he knew it Jeori was sitting in Interdimensional Travel...waiting.

~ ~ ~

Lance walked in with his arm around Ansel's shoulder. The boy took his seat silently. Lance looked around. "We are very fortunate to have Ansel back with us today. He has agreed to tell us the story of what happened to him four days ago. Please listen carefully, and take this all to heart. There are things out there that can be dangerous. In our excitement to explore we too often forget this. Ansel, will you please come to the front of the class? You may sit on the top of my desk if it makes you more comfortable."

The twelve-year-old moved up quickly and sat on the edge of the desk. He glanced at his four co-conspirators. His eyes looked tired. "First of all, thanks Lance for bringing me out. You probably saved my life." His teacher nodded.

"Okay...well, you know how the pattern starts," he began. "That part went fine. I went to my usual spot on Earth Two, to the bluff overlooking the ocean. I lay down. I decided to travel out to the cat planet. As some of you know, that's one of my favorite dem spots. I love how the cat people move and how they talk telepathically. They're so gentle and smart. It's fun to see them walking upright. And I love their clothes; the different colored and patterned vests and jackets and long coats...but no pants, of course. They always remind me of some old vid cartoons. And the way they can hold things in their paws with those long claws is really great, too.

Ansel took a deep breath. "Anyway...to the weird part.... I was outside and some of the cat people had just moved away from where I was standing and watching them. The light in the sky was starting to get dimmer, and I thought maybe I should get back. Then I saw something strange. There was a dark circle maybe two inches around floating in the air right behind where the cat people had been standing. They hadn't seemed to notice. What was it? I was curious and came closer. I could smell it. I know that seems strange, but the black hole—or whatever it was—smelled good... really, really good! It smelled just like a pine forest. So I went right up to investigate."

And suddenly...it swallowed me. That is the only way I can put it. I was inside the hole...inside the darkness. I couldn't get out! I tried to move forward, but with every step I took, the darkness got more and more intense. So I stopped. I began to feel really trapped. And it was as if the darkness liked that. I could feel it pushing on me from all sides like some kind of animal nudging me. I was stuck. And I was cold...so very cold. And the smell that had seemed so good at first had suddenly gone rotten." A single tear rolled down Ansel's cheek.

"That is enough, Ansel. I know it is difficult to replay what happened, but I think you understand why it is an important story for your classmates to hear." The boy nodded weakly and returned to his seat.

"Ansel first told me his story two days ago while he was recovering in the healing center. Something sounded familiar so I went back to Admin to check the outtake file of one Kadrun Connelly. Any of you remember Kad?" There was a nod from every head. Jeori leaned in closer.

"As you may or may not be aware of, anytime a student decides to leave one learning center for another there is an outtake interview given. I have called over and received Kadrun's permission to read you one section of his report. You may find this interesting."

Lance picked up a sheet of paper and began to read. *"Everyone who knows I'm leaving thinks it's because I am sick of doing art. Well, that's what I told them, and it's partially true. I want to try something different. But the main reason is that I want to get into a pod that doesn't have Interdimensional Travel class. I know everyone here thinks dem traveling is such a great way to inspire new art. But it can be dangerous. I didn't tell anyone this because they'd think I was weirder than they already do. But one day I was traveling out from class...thank goodness I was in class and not doing this on my own...when I smelled this great forest smell...."*

"From here," Lance continued, "the story plays out very much like Ansel's telling. The only difference was that Kad was able to come back when he heard my familiar voice pattern calling everyone out. And another disturbing fact—this didn't happen on the cat planet. He was on a different planet in the seventh dimension of the Pleiadian belt."

Jeori groaned. *This thing could be anywhere??*

~ Chapter 23 ~

Lance Kartoofle took a moment to stare out the classroom window toward the center of the quad. He ran a hand distractedly through his sandy hair and turned back toward his students, his blue eyes intense.

"Because of this new and rather disturbing development, I am obviously wondering at the best way to proceed. There is the option of canceling Interdimensional Travel for the indefinite future...."

Jeori's hand popped up. "But Lance...doesn't that mean that more kids would just be curious enough to try going out on their own? And you wouldn't be there to help if something went wrong."

"Jeori has made a good point here. And once word of what has happened gets spread around the pod as it will—like lightning, I suspect.... No, I see that canceling the class is not the answer. This would only encourage more students to go searching for this thing, whatever it is."

Ansel raised his hand. "I never felt anything like it before. When I was trapped in the dark, and whatever that was pushed against me, it didn't hurt. That wasn't the problem. There was an icky energy that started in my chest and stomach and took me over."

"Ah, yes, Ansel. What you felt was quite prevalent on Old Earth. I believe that what you felt was *fear*."

Around the class heads nodded. In one way or another all the students had felt a bit of this, whether they were nervous about the outcome of a project or running out of time to get their work done before an upcoming show.

"So," Lance continued "do any of you have ideas about how best to proceed? Yes...Michiko?"

"Maybe we each could get a code word to bring out a friend who might get stuck. You know...something that would work on anyone."

Jeori stuck his hand up wiggling his fingers. "But see, that's not the inside of the problem, is it? The big thing is how can we stop this from happening? Suppose this thing just appears somewhere and without anyone smelling that piney smell and moving closer, it comes forward and gobbles someone right up? What about that?"

Everyone started talking at once. The noise level in the room rose higher and higher. Finally Lance held up a hand and mind shouted *Stop!*

A smile flickered across Jeori's features. *Whew...I sure heard that!*

"All right. This is what we'll do. Give me the weekend to do some investigation at the Old Earth Library, Central Division. I suspect that the clue we are looking for might well be found"—he looked dramatically around the room—"in the past. We will meet again at our regular time on Tuesday and move forward from there. See what you can do until then to not encourage undue curiosity. I have the unfortunate suspicion that the only way out may be *in*," he added cryptically. "Class dismissed."

~ Chapter 24 ~

As the students from Interdimensional Travel were awakening on Saturday and trying to figure out just how they could make it through the weekend and Monday without spilling everything, Professor Lance Kartoofle was taking a seat on Lavender Line Air Transit.

What awaited the young man in the central region of the country was perhaps the largest library of Old Earth books and vids anywhere, certainly in Amerada and probably in the whole world. Hopefully there he would find the answers he sought.

In a bit less than an hour the mid-speed Lavender Line would carry Lance from his pod in the far west—approximately twenty miles inland from the shores of the Pacific Ocean near the town of Auburn, California—to the area of Moose Jaw, Saskatchewan. The White Line A.T. could make the same trip in a mere fifteen minutes. But the faster ride would have run through Lance's work credits at an alarming rate, and he didn't feel it was worth it.

The young man glanced down at the webbing barely visible beneath his skin. When he had walked through the A.T. scanner moments before, the red light had blinked showing credits being subtracted from his total. Since everything you needed for a good life was either provided outright in your pod or shared or borrowed from within the quad or from neighboring quads, if you stayed at home working your credits just kept on accumulating.

Lance realized that he had not traveled outside of his own community in a long while. And he had been so busy that he had barely noticed. In fact this was the first time he had used up any credits in nearly two years. How long had it been since he had taken a real vacation? He had more than enough credits for a big trip, even to Eurasia or Africa, especially if he teleported part of the way.

Perhaps after the solution was found to this potentially disastrous situation with interdem travel, it would be a good time to take a break from teaching. Lydia had been a professor at Art Pod at least as long as he had, and as far as he knew she hadn't been taking time off either. So perhaps....

But this was speculation. Lance had less than an hour to access the maps of Old Earth Library and get a feel for the areas he would explore. He wasn't sure why he had to hold the actual old world books in his hands and read them directly rather than getting the information straight off his computer. But the feeling was strong and he followed it.

Lance lifted the small flap on the seat back in front of him and with his thumb touched the gel pad depression. His name and identifying information appeared on the screen as the small on board computer lit up. Lance pulled a fresh mind tab from his shirt pocket, unwrapped the small delicate square carefully, and secured it behind his left ear. He was now linked to the computer. He thought the beginning commands and located "Old Earth Library, Central Div." He thought the key words—*dark, fear,* and *black hole.* References immediately scrolled onto the screen.

"Black hole" took Lance to books and vids about gravitational pull, neutron stars...all astronomy references. No, from Ansel's description this wasn't what he was looking for. The word "dark" got him into some of the same reference points—"dark matter" among them. A possibility, he guessed, but yet the feeling of being nudged as if by an animal didn't fit. Besides if what was going on had something to do with dark matter, Lance knew he was way out of his element.

Then the word "fear" began to scroll out references. My Goodness! There were an amazing number of references to fear within the Old Earth Library, too many even to count! Lance shook his head. Old Earth was a truly frightening place. He cross referenced "fear" with the subsets "black" and "dark" and finally felt as if he had hit on something. At least it was a place to start.

~ Chapter 25 ~

For the students in Lance's Interdimensional Travel class, the weekend passed in an uneasy blur. Each of the fifteen tried to move normally through the next few days and to keep their thoughts strictly neutral. This was not an easy thing to do. Many either took to staying in their rooms as much as possible or to taking long walks which would get them away from Art Pod.

On Sunday afternoon Kayla knocked briefly on Jeori's door and not waiting for an answer poked her head into his room. Her friend was hard at work on a poster for parents' weekend.

"So what's going on?" the girl asked as she entered his room and walked over to the desk where he was working.

Jeori didn't look up. "Just finishing this poster," he answered quickly and held it up. "Do you like it?"

"Don't try to cover this up, Jeori Kellogg! There is something going on. I've felt the buzz of it in the cafeteria and in the hallways and on the grounds. It has something to do with your class and dem popping. I know that much. So tell me!"

Jeori sighed and looked into his friend's eyes. "All right...I'll tell you. But you better be as good at blocking as you are at listening in on other people's thoughts. Sit down."

Kayla smoothed the rumpled cover on Jeori's bed and sat.

"Here it is, but I won't say it out loud." There was a minute of quiet. "And that about wraps it up," Jeori finished.

"Do you know what? You did pretty good blocking that all this time. I'm proud of you."

"You are?"

"Yep. I knew something was up, but that's all. In the past I have been able to hear your thoughts like they were my own."

Jeori smiled. This was good news. "You won't spread this around, will you?"

"I promise. But I suspect everyone will know the whole story pretty soon anyway. The only good thing is, considering what happened to your friend, I don't think anyone will try to go out and find that dark place or whatever it is right away."

The boy nodded. "At least there's that."

"I have an idea!" Kayla said with excitement in her voice. "I've wanted to try this out for awhile anyway. Let's go down to the lounge...."

"But...." Jeori began.

"My plan is simple. If I can block my thoughts so no one can hear what I'm thinking, maybe I can block yours as well."

"Woo! I hadn't thought of that."

"Come on! Let's get you out of this room and try it out."

Sudden whispered conversation and meaningful looks followed Kayla and Jeori as they entered the student lounge.

"He was there," a voice said from across the room. Then silence.

The two friends sat down on one end of the long couch that fronted the fireplace. "What do I do?" Jeori whispered. "They already know."

"But not the details," she said in a soft voice. "That's what they want. Hush!"

Jeori took a deep breath and picked up a vid book about African art that was sitting on the table in front of him. He began by scanning the video output on the first page and reading—well, pretend reading the second page. The stares from nearby students were making real reading impossible. He glanced up. People were shaking their heads and turning away. *It's working*, Jeori thought.

Shush! Let me concentrate.

Jeori continued pretending to read, clicking the vid pages one to the next. He could feel a wall of white noise surrounding him like a blanket. He could also feel students all around the room trying to break through the block.

A bell chimed. "Time for dinner! Let's go," Kayla said and smiled with satisfaction.

The two friends sprinted for the cafeteria leaving the returning buzz of conversation far behind them.

~ Chapter 26 ~

"Excellent! Simply excellent!" Kayla crowed as the two friends followed the delicious aroma of fried chicken and twice baked potatoes to the food line. They grabbed empty trays and watched them filled.

"Stay near me at dinner, Jeori, and I'll do it again." They moved to an empty table and put down their trays.

"I have an even better idea," Kayla said under her breath. "I want to expand the block. Do you see any more of your dem popping crew?"

Jeori looked around. He could just make out Jake's curly black hair on the other side of the cafeteria.

Right! Now I'll send him the message to join us.

Jeori turned toward Kayla, his eyes full of happy surprise. *I heard your thought!*

Deep in concentration, Kayla only nodded. A moment later, Jake made his way over to their table. It appeared that Jeori's partner in crime was having problems of his own. Several of the older students were shadowing him, moving as he moved across the cafeteria. It was obvious that he had been trying not to think about you-know-what with only partial success.

"Where's everybody else?" Jeori questioned in a low voice as his fellow dem popper lowered his tray to the table and sat down.

"My guess is they took some food upstairs to their rooms," Jake answered in an equally soft tone.

The students who had been following took empty spots at several nearby tables and leaned in as if to listen. Jake looked at Kayla with suspicion.

Jeori whispered, "Oh, she's okay, Jake. Jake, this is my good friend, Kayla. She's the one who called you over and she has my complete trust...if you know what I mean."

Hi, Jake, Kayla thought. *I know what's going on. You can trust me. I'm going to help. Pretend everything is normal. Say something to Jeori. Say anything at all.*

"Mind if I sit with you guys?" I've been working all day on my poster for parents' day. Did you finish yours, Jeori?"

"Still working on it," Jeori replied taking a bite of potato. "Mm...this potato is really good. And this chicken is just the way I like it...all crispy."

Jake raised his eyebrows and looked carefully at Kayla. *What are ...? Are you blocking me?*

The girl nodded and said aloud, "I didn't get to do a poster this time since I did one last term for Parents' Day. Are you doing it as part of Chakra Colors?"

"Yep...I'm still working on my yellow...a large acrylic painting. I seem to take forever to get through each color set, but I'm sure having fun." *What is she doing? I feel like I'm sitting in cotton.*

You know what she's doing. She's blocking all three of us at once. Fantasmic, huh? Surprise filled Jeori's face, and he laughed out loud. The spying students turned and looked at him.

I'm getting it Kayla!

Yes, that's really great. Now I'm going to try to put a hold on this energy so it will work automatically. I shouldn't have to try so hard.

"There, that's better!" Kayla said aloud. She got some strange looks from the same students who had obviously been trying to listen in without success.

Now we are the only ones who can hear each other when we mind speak. And Jeori! Welcome to the club! I'd bet you can test out of beginning telepathy class with no problem now.

Do you really think so?

Well just look at what you're doing! You're picking up every thought I'm thinking!

I am, aren't I? Jeori was so excited he was practically in tears.

After dinner Kayla took the boys upstairs to her room where she gave them some tips on blocking their thoughts more effectively. After an hour of practice on each other, they were getting really good. Jeori could hardly believe how easy it seemed all of a sudden.

And now they were ready for Monday.

~ Chapter 27 ~

The new student took a seat with most of the others near the back of the classroom. He was wearing fresh blue jeans and the pod standard, a tee shirt with the Actors' Guild logo on the front and "Act Out!" stamped in large letters on the back. His shirt was red, the letters white. He chuckled and received some pointed stares as he looked around at his new classmates. Most were years younger and nearly all were wearing black on black. He sensed that some had chosen black because everybody else was wearing it. But a few...well, they reminded him of himself.

The fifteen-year-old thought about how he used to feel wearing black...different, special, and somehow safe. Black had always seemed a place he could crawl into...a place where no one could see him...no one could see the sad child who had been left behind, and who was trying so desperately not to care about that.

A voice broke into his thoughts. "We have a student new to the Actors' Pod joining us today," said Magnum Potate, the aging professor who for years had taught all the beginning acting courses. "Kadrun Connelly is most recently from Art Pod. I have been following this young man's art for several years, and I would suggest a trip to the Main Gallery if you haven't had the pleasure. Kadrun's style in the various mediums is unique, simple, and unforgettable. And now to increase his range, he will immerse himself in the art of acting. Welcome Kad. Is that what you wish to be called?"

Kad nodded, a bit stunned by what this old professor, whom he had never seen in his life, had just said. He tried to wipe the smile off his face as he looked around. When was the last time he had felt there was anything to smile about?

Just one student sat right up front in the smallish classroom. She seemed to be about ten, and there was no slumping with this girl. She did not wear black, but instead had chosen faded blue jeans and a royal blue tee with "Act Out!" in lime green letters.

Professor Potate was addressing her now. "Phoebe, would you please take a few moments to explain to our new classmate our ongoing assignment and the reason for such?"

"Sure! Hi Kad!" the girl said in a confident voice, turning around further in her seat to look him in the eye. Kad nodded. "So here it is. Some kids don't like this at first, but I bet you will as you get used to it."

What is she talking about?

"That's exactly where I'm going, you see. What I'm talking about is that we have to keep a running diary of our thoughts nearly every day. No! Don't get excited. I get what you're feeling, but really there's nothing to worry about. This is just for you if you want it to be. You can block it to the moon if you want to. The reason to do this assignment is that Professor Potate says we need to understand the motivations of the characters we encounter to play them well. This means...why do they do what they do? And to play other parts convincingly we need to understand our own motivations...why we do the things we do. Get it?"

Kadrun took a deep breath and nodded. Oh, yeah, he understood all right.

"Thank you, Phoebe. Now class, I know that a good many of you have been enjoying playing it safe in the back of the room. But we have good news! A larger room has just opened up. Please stand, gather your things, and follow me!

Kad felt like one of a family of baby ducklings following Mommy Duck as he joined the line of students making their way down the long hall. He entered the new classroom to find just the right number of chairs placed in a circle. A smile touched his lips as he heard the internal groans from most of his new classmates.

Kadrun's Diary

Monday

Well, hello dearest diary. I'm gonna write in you, and you're gonna be just what I make you—get it? I have to do this so let's get down to it.

So today I started my very first class in Actors' Pod. It's called "Life as a Play." I have no idea where we're going. It could be good or not. But the professor has the weirdest name I've ever heard...Magnum Potate. Can you believe it???!! He is a surprise. He's old and probably nearing transition. Never mind. He pays attention. I felt like he knew me right away...maybe from my art. He liked it.

I see myself in some of these kids wearing black. They act like they don't care about much of anything. And other kids think they're dark and mysterious—been there. I wonder how many of them had mothers who screamed in their heads so the child wouldn't hear and fathers who said mostly "Err...yes, dear...okay," and backed away. Mom never got that I heard every one of her thoughts. What did she expect? I was her kid, wasn't I?

Wednesday

Today was a surprise. Prof. Potate—uh, Magnum—he said we could call him that—started a deck of cards going around the circle. We were supposed to take one without looking and pass the rest. Then we could look.

I got a card that said "Pansy Needy" on it. There was a picture of Pansy on the front and a line of her dialogue on the back. I recognized the artist at once! This was Jill's project in Game Creation class last year. I took the class, too. I created a board game. And yeah, I was "bored" by my own game. (Hey...is that some kind of message??)

Jill's okay. She treated me like I was normal. Anyway, I knew she was working on a game of some sort with a prof from Actors' Guild, but I didn't know who. Maybe I'll visit Art Pod sometime and tell her that we used her cards.

So anyway...here's what we did. We read the bit of dialogue on the back of the card in whatever voice seemed right for our character. On my first card Pansy Needy said this: "Nobody wants to be my friend. I know what they're saying. Why is my life so unfair?"

Then we had to—quick without thinking it over— describe our characters mom or dad to the rest of the class. This was actually fun. We were all laughing. Even the "blackest of the blacks" was laughing their heads off!!

Sunday

This is the private diary of Kadrun Connelly! For My Eyes ONLY! ALL OTHERS KEEP OUT!!!!

So in some ways I am my mother's child...and my father's, too. They are both telepaths. But that's where it ends.

*Mother never loved Father, while he loved her so much...
at first anyway. The problem began when Doreen, who would
become "Mom,"—I laugh at that—decided she had to have
a baby. See, she was mad because her best friend Alice fell in
love with this guy visiting from another pod. And soon IT
happened. Alice and Bill decided to take the classes and get
the license to make a baby. Doreen was furious because she
loved Alice. She didn't want anything or anyone to come
between them. I heard this from her thoughts.*

*Anyway, Doreen decided she would take the courses
and get the license, too. That way she and Alice could study
together and have their babies together and raise them in the
same neighborhood. But she had a problem...no man to be
the father. She looked around. Jeremy had been asking her
out for awhile, and she knew he liked her. So the next time he
asked, she said yes. They went on one date and then another
and another. She pretended to fall in love. Soon they were
taking the classes and preparing to be parents. She was a
good actor and good at blocking her thoughts, too. Jeremy
didn't have a clue. The four of them studied together, and the
two women got pregnant within a few weeks of each other.*

*But before the two babies were even born, Alice
announced that she and Bill were moving to live near his pod
on the other side of the country. Doreen was outraged! Her
best friend was deserting her, and here she was stuck with a
man she didn't love and the baby she really only wanted as a
prop in the first place.*

*Then I was born. After four and a half miserable years
of listening to what they were thinking, I was finally dropped
off at Ladybug Playhouse with phony smiles and "It's better
for you this way." I'm sure they separated and went on with
their lives, but I haven't heard. Dad did come to visit me once
about a year after they left me. He didn't have much to say
and acted embarrassed and uncomfortable to be there. It was
a relief when he left.*

2065

The weird thing is I don't think either of them ever figured out that I was listening in on every one of their angry and hurt thoughts. I don't blame my father so much. He was duped and then broken up. But how could she carry me in her belly and then have me and not care at all?? I guess the only good thing is that I got so much practice listening and blocking when I lived with them that I can hear anyone's thoughts and block so well now that no one knows I'm doing it. Yippee. Thanks Mom. Thanks Dad.

~ Chapter 28 ~

Kad's Diary

Friday

Sometimes I think that Magnum is looking straight into my life with what he gives us to do. Today's homework— we're supposed to make up a new past for ourselves. And not just any past but the happiest, the most perfect past we can imagine. He told us first to think of how we'd like to be right now if we could be any way we wanted. What new roles would we play? What qualities would we possess?

Next we're to imagine what our lives would have been like to create that person. He said we should create our new pasts very clearly in our minds for ten minutes with as many colorful details as we can think of. And he warned us not to picture any of our old pasts...that this would "ruin the bouquet." Those were his words. After ten minutes of experiencing our new pasts, we are supposed to open our eyes and feel any difference in energy and in how we feel now. Then we have to journal our results and share as much as we want for the next class.

Saturday

So here is my new past. Mom and Dad are different. No! Strike this! Mom and Dad are both strong and happy people. Dad is a popular teacher at Western Division Geography Pod and Mom is...yes! She's a clothing designer and costume maker in Fiber Arts in ...yeah, Eastern Division. She's far away.

Doreen and Jeremy first met at the Winter Solstice Festival of Lights Dance. He introduced himself to her and swung her around on the dance floor all night. Soon they fell deeply in love. Then they decided to make a baby. They had so much fun taking the courses. They got the license. Mom sang to me every day for the nine months I was inside of her. So even before I was born I could feel her love for me. And Mom and Dad laughed a lot. I could hear that before I was born, too!

So I was born a very happy baby. When I was old enough, Dad would carry me around on his shoulders, and Mom would make chocolate chip cookies and cut up sandwiches in funny shapes for me. Mom loved to plant flowers, so our yard was full of color. She would sing songs as she worked, and she would let me dig in the dirt with my little shovel and pull weeds and even plant tiny seeds. Mom and Dad would also take me with them when they put in their time at the community garden. They let me pull up the carrots and radishes and pick strawberries to bring home.

Of course part of the time when I was a toddler, I went to our local playhouse in the mornings, and that was fun, too. Mz. Keller was always smiling and there were lots of toys and paints and stuff to do. I made some good friends there, and some of them I still connect with by comp though we live far away from each other. When I was nine I got to choose where I would live and study next. I like art, but I decided on Actors' Pod because I love to act. I'm going to be a famous actor on stage and vid. Life is good!

Tuesday Night

Outtakes: Ten minutes of this exercise was not enough! I went on for fifteen at least, and the pictures got even clearer than what I just wrote. I filled in the colors like in a painting. I kept looking at the smiles on my parents' faces and hearing their laughter. Finally I opened my eyes. Was my room brighter?? Yes, I think it was. And I felt lighter, like something slow and dark was moving out and away from me.

Now a few days later I still feel different. I think about my new past a lot. It's like my old past and my new past are both here in my mind, but the new past is becoming the stronger one. And that dark feeling is still mostly gone. I know this is good for me to do. What good does it do concentrating on the bad stuff, anyway? Sometimes now I catch myself smiling at nothing at all.

Phoebe came up to me in the hall today and just stared at me. Then she raised her eyebrows. Suddenly we were both laughing! Of course she had done the exercise, too. I think she went for more silliness and less of being Miss Perfect all the time. Yeah, this is good stuff. What will I be now??

Wednesday night

So I walked into Life as a Play today thinking I'd surprise everyone. I was a bit late, 'cause I had to grab new clothes in my size from the hall cabinet before I could get dressed. For the first time ever I decided to dress totally in white—even white running shoes. Bash idea, huh? I entered class and looked around. Nearly every one of my "dark and mysterious" classmates was wearing...Can you guess what I'm going to say??—They were wearing white on white!!

Sunday

Dear Diary,
Did you know that Kadrun is actually a fun guy? No! Not a mushroom—a fun-gi! Get it? Yuck! Yuck! I am just such a character. And not just in my classes. Weird thing is as I'm pretending to be this new someone, this happy and outgoing person, things are changing. Kids are beginning to come up and poke me in the shoulder if they're tall enough—or in the

2065

side like I'm one of them. If only the students from Art Pod could see me now!

~ Chapter 29 ~

Kadrun Black sat at the cafeteria table half listening to one of his new friends practicing the part of the Egyptian Cow God, Hathor, greeting the dead. Kad had ironically taken to using the last name of "Black" soon after he had stopped wearing it. Today he was dressed in his current favorite; light blue faded jeans, white canvas sneakers, and a white hooded sweatshirt with words "Act Out" stamped in purple on the back.

Something was going on at his old pod. There were rumors...something about dem popping and danger...a student getting into trouble as he was traveling out interdimensionally. Kadrun shivered. He had more than a good idea what this was about. Lance's quick phone call asking permission to share some of Kad's outtake interview now made perfect sense. He had been so busy practicing lines for his upcoming monologue that he had said "Sure, sure, whatever" without really paying attention to what his former teacher was asking.

Kadrun was curious. In one way he wanted to find out more. Could what happened to him have happened to someone else? It would be a simple matter to walk across the quad and wander through the halls listening in. He might even run into Cleo. But...in another way he didn't want to go anywhere near Art Pod yet. He wouldn't risk that hungry darkness finding him again. And so far he had been safe here. He was having weird dreams, but mostly they dissolved as soon as he woke up. Anyway there was probably no connection.

2065

~ ~ ~

Meanwhile over at Art Pod lunch period was just ending, and kids were streaming out of the cafeteria. Only two students remained. The boy and girl were hunched over at one of the back tables talking quietly.

"Lance should have been back by now, Kayla," Jeori said with a worried frown. "He promised he'd be here by this morning, but I checked around. No one has seen him. And I have his class this afternoon."

"I'm sure he's okay, Jeori. Maybe he just found more information than he expected, and it took him a little longer." She studied her friend's face. He looked worn out.

Kayla stood. "I've got to go," she said rather apologetically. "I have to grout my mosaic stepping stone today. We're supposed to place our stones outside in only two days so they'll be ready for parents' weekend, and they have to be totally dry before we can do that. Don't you have swimming next period?"

"Uh, yeah...right. I do," Jeori answered shaking his head. He stood and headed for the locker room.

An hour of mostly practicing movements for the butterfly stroke was just too much. Jeori was done in. He hadn't been sleeping well the last few nights, and if his next class had been anything except Interdimensional Travel he might have skipped it. He had learned early on that the teachers didn't care if you showed up for classes or not. And since the subjects were interesting, and you completed most assignments at your own pace, there was nearly complete attendance for every session. But if you had something special happening or didn't feel well, it was no problem to miss a period or even a day of school.

Jeori reached his classroom to find a few of his fellow students talking quietly in the hall. "No Lance?" he asked. Sonia shook her head and pointed to the closed door. A note was taped to its center.

Prof. Kartoofle delayed.
I. T. cancelled today.

"Have any of you seen Ansel?" Jeori asked looking around. There was a shaking of heads. No, no one had seen him. The last Jeori had seen of him was on Saturday. And the eleven-year-old hadn't looked right.

Jeori sighed. A free period.... This would be good. He pulled himself up the stair railing and headed for his room. Taking off his shoes and throwing them by the door, Jeori flopped down on his bed. "Just a few minutes rest...." He yawned.

Jeori was asleep immediately. So he missed the moment when a small black hole winked into existence on the wall opposite his bed...and just as quickly disappeared.

~ ~ ~

There was a loud knocking on the door. "Jeori... Jeori, are you in there?"

"Huh? What is it?"

Kayla popped her head in. "You missed your studio time is all. One of the kids in your class stopped me in the hall to ask if you were all right. Your dem popping adventures are getting around, Jeori. Everyone's talking about what they think happened now. Some have got it almost right."

The boy groaned and pulled out of bed. He yawned loudly. "What time is it?"

"It's nearly suppertime. Are you okay?"

Jeori shivered. He was all sweaty. "I'm not sure. Did Lance ever show up? I think I need to talk to him."

"Why?" Kayla came further into the room. She looked at her friend more closely. "Have you been crying? Your cheeks are all wet. Did something happen?"

Jeori shook his head to clear it. "I've just been having the weirdest dreams, Kayla. This last one was the worst yet. This time I was trapped and squeezed between two pieces of glass. I could see through the glass, but I couldn't move. A huge eye was staring down at me. And I swear...the center of it was a...a deep black hole." He shivered again.

"And that's not the first either. Saturday night when I was dreaming, I saw the blank white screen in front of my face. I was about to walk through it to switch dimensions when a black circle appeared right in the center of it. I backed up and grabbed the screen carefully from the outsides. It had turned into paper, and I crumpled it up so the blackness couldn't get to me. But when I tried to throw the paper into the trash, it stuck to my hand. No matter what I tried I couldn't get it off. When I woke up my blankets were twisted all around me.

"Then last night I had another one. And this one started out just fine. There was a pretty little pine tree that I was about to decorate for the holidays. It smelled so fresh and good. I reached into a bag and started pulling out ornaments. Every one of them was the same. They were eyes made out of glass. I started hanging them on the tree one after the other until the tree was full of eyes. And then I swear...one of them blinked at me."

He sighed. "Normally I have really good dreams, but these dreams all began with me feeling kind of normal and ended up with me feeling really scared. I have a bad feeling that this is all connected somehow."

Kayla nodded her head. "I think you're right. You do need to talk to Lance and to the rest of your dem popping crew, too. Maybe you're not the only one this is happening to."

"Yeah, I'm thinking maybe this might be what's going on with Ansel. You go down to dinner and see if you can spot him. You know who he is, right?" Kayla nodded. "Okay. If he starts to leave go tell him to wait for me. Tell him it's important. I'll meet you there in a bit. I need a shower."

~ ~ ~

The shower felt wonderful. Jeori foamed himself up good and just stood there for a few minutes letting the hot water run down his body and carry all his bad dreams down the drain. He dried, wrapped himself in his purple towel, and rushed back to his room to dress. He knew he'd better hurry if he didn't want to miss dinner.

~ Chapter 30 ~

Luckily there were still students in line and plenty of food left when Jeori got to the cafeteria. He grabbed a tray and watched as his plate was filled with his very favorite dinner—spaghetti and meatballs, garlic bread and salad—and the usual cup of milk.

He spotted Kayla, hurried over, and sat down at her table. Several of their friends moved over to make room for him. "So...have you seen Ansel?" he asked around a big mouthful of spaghetti. He took a bite of the crunchy bread. "M-m-m-m.... This tastes so good!"

"Yes, he's here." Kayla looked at her friend strangely. "Did you eat enough today, Jeori? I've never seen you so hungry."

""I don't know why, Kayla," the boy mumbled shoveling one bite of salad and then another into his mouth, "but I'm starving. And this is probably the best food I've ever tasted." He continued eating as fast as he possibly could.

"When you get a chance," his friend continued as Jeori jabbed another bite of pasta and twisted it around his fork, "you might want to take a look over there." She nodded her head toward the back wall. There was Ansel all right, and although every other table in the cafeteria was crowded, he was sitting all by himself. Jeori glanced at Ansel quickly and was about to take another bite.

"Wha...." Jeori's fork fell to the table. "Do you see it Kayla? Do you see what's around Ansel?"

"Yeah, I sure do...and so does everyone else in the room. You do notice that no one is feeling brave enough to sit with him."

"This is bad. That dark cloud of energy.... Oh, this is a very bad sign. Lance has simply got to be here now. He's just got to."

As if on cue, Jeori's phone rang. He pulled it out of his pocket. He flipped it open. The screen said "Professor Kartoofle." Yes! It was his teacher. "Lance! Lance! You need to...." Jeori began. He listened. It was a recorded message. He listened a moment longer and then slowly closed and pocketed the phone. "He wants the whole class to meet in his room at nine sharp tomorrow morning," Jeori said in flat voice. "That's no good," Jeori said wiping his face with his napkin and standing up. "It's not soon enough for Ansel." He took a deep breath. "I'm going over."

"Wait! I'm coming, too."

"Thank you, Kayla. You're a real good friend."

~ ~ ~

As they approached the far table, Jeori looked around for reinforcements, but he couldn't spot any of the others involved in last week's dem popping incident. However, some students at the nearby tables were openly staring at them.

"Dang," Jeori cursed under his breath. A moment later he stopped directly in front of Ansel and said in an overly cheerful voice, "Hi, Ansel! This is Kayla. Can we sit with you?"

"Yeah, sure...I guess so."

The two sat down and in a softer tone Jeori continued. "I need to talk with you, and Kayla's excellent at blocking. She'll take care of that part." He nodded at Kayla, and she began to block anyone listening in on their whispered conversation with a strong sending of white noise. "You've got some weird energy around you, Ansel. Did you know that?"

"No. I can't see anything...but I don't feel so good." He looked down at the table. "I just know that nobody wants to sit with me." Tears filled his eyes. "I didn't do anything wrong."

"I know you didn't, Ansel. Listen. I've been having really strange dreams lately...bad dreams...about eyes and stuff...."

Ansel snuffed, grabbed a tissue out of his pocket, and blew his nose. He looked up. "You have?"

"Yeah, eyes and black holes and I can't move. I've had three dreams like that so far."

"And you can't get away, right? Every time I go to sleep I have them...ever since *it* happened and I left the healing center." He shivered. "And now I'm afraid to go to sleep, and I almost can't wake up if I do get to sleep. You've really seen them, too...the eyes?"

"Yeah...and this is important. We have to tell someone now and get some help. Come on! If we can't find Lance, let's go find one of the grandmas or grandpas. They'll know what to do."

"I'll get rid of the trays," Kayla offered, "and you two go ahead. I think Grandma Leah might be up in her room."

~ ~ ~

All eyes in the cafeteria were on the two boys as they made their way toward the door. Meanwhile, directly above the table where they had just been sitting, an angry cloud of black filaments swirled in the air for a moment...and was gone.

~ Chapter 31 ~

Ansel and Jeori made their way up the stairs and straight to Grandma Leah's apartment at the end of the hall. Her door was open. The smell of sweet honey wafted out to greet the boys. Looking in they spotted a golden honeycomb candle burning brightly on the round table by Grandma's chair. Leah was standing there waiting for them.

"Ansel dear...and Jeori, please come in. It's so good to see you." She gave them both warm hugs. "Come sit down and tell me all about it. I know there's been some trouble lately, and especially for you two, isn't that right?" They nodded and sat down side-by-side on the small couch facing Grandma's recliner. She took a seat. A moment later Grandma's large tabby cat, Leo the Lion, padded in from the bedroom, jumped up onto her lap, and began licking his paws with great concentration.

The boys quickly filled in Grandma Leah with everything that had been happening—Ansel's near disaster on the cat planet, the dreams they'd both been having, and the black cloud that had surrounded Ansel at dinner. "And we can't find Lance," Jeori finished. "Is he home yet, Grandma?"

"I believe he's on his way, boys," she said, smiling slightly and looking toward the floor as she ran her hand distractedly down Leo's tawny back. "Yes, I sense him on Air Transit. At this very moment he's looking out at the night sky and the lights below him. And his thoughts are very busy with all that he has learned. It shouldn't be long now.

"But to tell you the truth, I don't think you should wait for him. He'll be tired himself, and by the looks of you two you both need some real rest more than anything else...some peaceful sleep without those dreams. Give me a moment."

Leah sat quietly for nearly a minute, stroking Leo's fur while her attention was elsewhere. The only sounds to be heard were the ticking of Grandma's antique wall clock and the cat's loud purring. "Very well," she said at last. "Light massages are arranged for each of you at the healing center, and two beds are being readied. After your massages the whirlpool bath and some sleep should set you up as good as new. Then you'll be fresh for your morning meeting with Lance. And don't worry about having bad dreams, my dears. The energies of the healing center won't allow for that kind of nonsense."

Relieved, the boys thanked Grandma Leah, each receiving another hug on their way out. They dashed first to their own rooms for pajamas and next to their bathrooms for their toothbrushes and combs. Jeori knocked on Kayla's door and quickly filled her in as he waited for Ansel to get back. He knew it would take a little longer for his friend since the rooms for the older students were on the higher floors. It was nearly dark when the two finally hurried down the path to the brightly lit, rounded building that housed Healing Arts.

~ ~ ~

It was the first time in his life that the eleven-year-old had ever gotten a massage. Jeori was in bliss. The lavender massage oil smelled wonderful, and the young intern's hands used just the right pressure on his back, legs, arms, neck, and scalp to help him relax. Next he showered to wash off the oil and again met up with Ansel in the whirlpool bath. They stayed in the swirling hot water until they were both red as lobsters and nearly asleep.

After donning pajamas and brushing their teeth, the boys were shown to their beds near the door of the large sleeping room. Only a few of the other beds were in use. Someone nearby was already snoring softly. They climbed in simultaneously pulling the soft feather filled comforters up over their shoulders.

Ansel turned toward Jeori and said in a sleepy voice, "I think we should just live here forever, Jeori. That would take care of it, don't you think?"

"Yeah...and get massages every day." Jeori sighed. "You think maybe we could be their mascot?"

"Rah, rah," Ansel replied softly. Jeori yawned loudly, and that was the very last sound out of the two boys until morning.

~ Chapter 32 ~

Miralandra, Captain of the Starship Sky Scraper

Ippsy Bobbinsford, She-Pirate of Outer Space

The Dullish Adventures of Victor and Veronica Escargot... exploring space at a snail's pace

Buzzy B. Goode and the Honeycomb Hairs, Beekeepers in Space

Ivonna Cream Soda

"No, no and NO! This simply isn't working." Kadrun chuckled weakly and sighed. "But I sure could use a cream soda." The tired student shook his head to clear it. He hadn't been sleeping well. That must be it. The assignment in Playwriting I had seemed so easy when Mz. Lipton handed it out:

"As the first part of this ongoing project, choose a title and create a simple sketch for a two act play. Set the stage and the storyline in Act 1, and show how the story might complete itself in Act 2. (This ending may be changed later.) Choose either comedy or drama. Due Wednesday."

The fifteen-year-old knew he wanted to do a comedy about outer space, and maybe even turn it into a musical later. He liked the idea of the main character being a woman, and he would love to play that part himself. He could dress in a shiny silver spacesuit and wear a blonde wig and high heels. Yes! That would be fun and unexpected. And the new Kadrun Black was all about having fun and doing the unexpected.

But it's Monday already, and I haven't even got the title yet let alone the story. Kad sighed. He slammed his notebook shut and closed his eyes a moment. It felt really good to close his eyes.

What...what was that? Kad's eyes flew open. He looked behind him. He looked at his closed door and then carefully around the rest of his room. He even studied the ceiling. Nothing! But just for a moment he had felt something...something watching him. He was sure of it.

It was definitely time to be somewhere else. Kad stood and took another quick glance around before shutting his door quietly behind him. He would go to the lounge where there would be bright lights and hopefully lots of people.

It can't get me there, he thought as he reached the end of the hall. He stopped dead in his tracks. "What can't get me there?" he said aloud. Without a backward glance, he hurried down the stairs.

~ ~ ~

Four students Kad knew from his classes waved hello as he made his way into the large brightly lit living room which was the social hub of Actors' Guild. Kad took a deep breath and felt something inside him release. He moved up to join an impromptu skit that was beginning in front of the fireplace.

"Little Gary Gorilla was lost in the big scary jungle," twelve-year-old Marilyn began in a little girl's voice. "He looked to the right and to the left and behind him, but it was no good. Mama Gorilla was nowhere to be found! But just then...."

"Just then," Kad continued, "a small but clever alien from the Quantum Realm of Arctus II popped his head out from behind a big green fern and said in a squeaky metallic voice, 'Hello Earthling. I seem to have misplaced my spaceship. Have you seen it?' Well, Gary Gorilla was sure surprised to see a little man in a silver suit talking to him so he..."

"He began making hooting noises and ran off through the jungle" added Jarvis, who was nine. "Then Gary Gorilla climbed a tree to look around some more for Mama Gorilla because he could see better from up there. He searched and searched, but he still could not find his sweet mama...."

"But what he did see," added Clive, another first year student, "was a shiny silver spaceship. Gary Gorilla knew this must be the alien's spaceship because even though he was a little gorilla, he was smart. He climbed back down the tree and ran back to find the alien. But what he found instead was..."

"Mama Gorilla! The End," finished a small girl whom Kad had never seen.

"Another!" Clive said. "Let's do more alien stuff!"

And so the play acting and laughter continued until general lights out at nine-thirty.

~ ~ ~

It had been a good diversion for Kad. But all too soon it was over, and it was time to return to his room... which seemed surprisingly neutral once he stepped inside. Everything seemed all right now. Kad changed to his pajamas and managed to make it down to the bathroom to brush his teeth before finally collapsing into bed. Hopefully tonight he would sleep better.

Chapter 33

It was one minute to nine. The whispering in the nearly filled classroom had begun three minutes earlier when someone had noticed that neither Ansel nor Jeori had arrived.

Professor Lance Kartoofle sat at his desk, his blue eyes shifting between his handheld comp and some papers laid out before him. At precisely nine o'clock he looked up and cleared his throat.

"As you may know, I returned last evening from the Old Earth Library. I apologize for missing yesterday's regular class period, but it was an enlightening trip to say the least, and I needed that bit of extra time. I will let you decide if the trip was worth it after you hear what I have to say. Is everyone present?"

As if on cue, two disheveled boys rushed into the room and hurried to their seats.

"Thank you for joining us Ansel and Jeori. You look well rested. Did you enjoy your overnight at Healing Pod?" Both boys blushed and nodded as the obvious question hit the rest of the class. *What were they doing in Healing Pod?*

"Before I begin with my story I need to ask. Have any of you been experiencing unusual and disturbing dreams of late?" Jeori and Ansel looked at each other and were about to raise their hands.

"I have," said a loud voice from the back of the room. The students turned around in their seats to see who had spoken. A gangly teenager stood in the doorway. He wore faded blue jeans and a white hooded sweatshirt with the hood pulled up. "I hope its okay I'm here," the teen said as he looked around the room. "I thought I just wanted to forget all about

Interdimensional Travel. See, I figured I'd be safe moving across the quad. But I was wrong. And this thing, whatever this is, it started with me. Some of you probably remember me. My name is Kadrun Black."

There was an audible gasp as everyone realized not only who this student was, but that Kad must have known all along the name that the students of Art Pod called him behind his back. And now he had taken "Black" as his last name. If a room could blush!

Kadrun pushed back his hood and looked around. "Don't worry about it," he said smiling. "I like the name...obviously." He moved into the room taking an empty seat near the front of the class. He slouched back in his chair and crossed one leg over the other.

Professor Kartoofle nodded. "Thank you for joining us Kadrun. I'm sure that your presence will help. Since we are all together now, let's begin. First I'd like a show of hands. How many of you have been having strange or uncomfortable dreams since the dem popping incident occurred?"

Immediately Jeori and Ansel and Kad raised their hands. Then Michiko's hand followed. There was a pause, and then around the room hands were being raised. Ansel turned to look at Jeori with a question in his eyes. *Some of them weren't even there.*

No they weren't, Jeori thought back. *What's going on?*

"This is unfortunately just as I suspected." Lance stood and began to pace back and forth in front of his desk. "I want to hear each of your stories, but first if you don't mind I'd like to introduce my trip to Old Earth Library. Oh, and before I forget, I want to remind each of you to avail yourselves of the Healing Guild's programs and beds if you find yourself unable to sleep peacefully before we get this situation sorted out. As Jeori and Ansel can tell you, it is a delightful place to find rest and rejuvenation.

"Now...where to begin? At the beginning I suppose. When I first entered the large double doors of Central Division Old Earth Library on Saturday, I was met by a skinny librarian with thinning gray hair who introduced himself as Randall. He offered to guide me to whatever sections I was interested in and asked what those might be.

"When I gave Randall the key words; *fear, dark,* and *black hole* a strange look came over his face.

"'Oh, yes of course,' the man said abruptly. 'Right this way.' We made our way quickly through several dimly lit corridors and stepped into a large chamber. Randall pointed to a section of bookshelves reaching to the high ceiling. The shelves were crammed with both books and vids. He motioned to an old fashioned sliding ladder poised against the wall for reaching the higher volumes. 'This is the major section you will want to look at,' he said briskly. 'And you've done quite well. You have only missed one key. Here, take this,' he said and handed me a small pager. 'If you have more requests, dial 24 and I or someone else will be here as soon as possible to help you.'

"I was about to ask which key he was referring to, when Randall turned on his heels and scooted down the hall away from me as fast as his spindly legs could carry him. I sent my thought out after him, but he didn't pause in his escape.

"Concerned, I looked around the large, empty room. I scanned it with my deeper senses for anything out of place. I could find nothing. I began pulling books off of the shelves following the key words. I was quickly amazed at the many references to fear. The number of fiction books alone was staggering.

And many people of Old Earth actually seemed to like feeling afraid if they were watching scary movies or reading frightening stories. I also discovered in these stories that fears often began in the dark."

Lance looked up. "Ansel, are you all right?"

"Sorry, Lance. I was just remembering. I'm okay. Go on."

"Very well.... I soon had a huge stack of books surrounding me on the table. I was so engrossed in what I was reading that I didn't notice when a woman sat down at the other end of the table. Finally I felt someone watching me. I looked up.

She was a big woman with short, curly black hair and deep brown skin. Her dark eyes held both worry and curiosity as she looked across at me and then at the books piled high around me. We began speaking mind to mind and quickly discovered we were on exactly the same search.

"You see, Lula teaches Interdimensional Travel in the Southern Division Physics Pod. And it turns out that the very same thing that has occurred here has happened to three of her students traveling to other planets and in different dimensions...first the good forest smell and then the dark and inescapable tunnel. Librarian Randall's behavior suggested that earlier visitors to the Central Library may have had the very same concerns—that something might have happened in the library or perhaps in Randall's dreams to cause *him* to feel afraid as well."

Everyone started whispering. Lance raised his hand in the air for quiet.

"Lula and I began working together, and I'm sure we got further as a team than we could have on our own. I tried using the pager a few times as questions arose, but no one ever came.

"So the first thing Lula and I did was to share our key words. She had already discovered the fourth key. Can any of you guess what that might be?"

Jeori raised his hand. "It's got to be *eye* or *eyes*, doesn't it? Or it could be *staring eye*...or...or...."

Lance looked around the room. "Or *evil eye*," he stated dramatically.

~ Chapter 34 ~

Jeori's Journal

Wednesday night

Our meeting with Lance was very strange. We got to share our dreams before he even told us what he and Lula discovered. Ansel and I weren't the only ones who dreamed about eyes. It turns out that everyone else in our dem popping crew did— Allie and Michiko and Jake as well as me and Ansel. And five others in class and Kad, too, have been having either dreams of eyes or the feeling that something was watching them. We talked about the black cloud that was around Ansel in the cafeteria, and how weak he felt when that was happening. We were all shivering by the end.

Oh, and Kad told us his whole story, too. From listening to him and later from what Ansel said, we maybe figured out why they had been targeted first. Yeah, that's the word Lance used...targeted. See, it was because they had been feeling unhappy and that's why the fear could get to them first. Lance said we all have to pay more attention to our feelings.

He told us stuff about Old Earth that I'd never heard— about all the things that people felt afraid of back then— death and enemies and war and disease and accidents and not having a nice place to live or good clothes to wear or enough food to eat. He talked about people stealing money from each other and killing people and prisons where you threw people who did bad things, and how that only made them meaner. See ...there were so many things on Old Earth to be afraid of. But what do we have to make us afraid now? Not much, eh?

Lance and Lula figured that the Evil Eye and darkness were used to make us feel afraid because our ancestors carried those fears through many lifetimes. The idea of the Evil Eye was that you could be cursed when someone who wanted to hurt you just stared at you really hard. Then you would have bad luck and maybe even keel over and die! Belief in the Evil Eye was found in lots of different cultures all over the world for a very long time. So whoever was doing this knew that somewhere in our DNA, in our cellular memories—that's what Lance said—we carry a receptor for these fears. He said a receptor is like a mitt when you play baseball. And fear is the ball.

Kad's Diary

Wednesday night

I didn't think I wanted to go, but I felt what was happening and found myself walking across the quad anyway. It turns out that Lance had called me with his mind to see if I would get the message. He told me after. Anyway, I showed up in Interdimensional Travel just as they were starting. They didn't even recognize me at first! I told them my name. Dear journal, I wish I had a vid of their faces!

Anyway, the stories came out about the dreams and bad feelings so many of us have been having. But why did it all start with Ansel and me? Lance said fear can only take hold where there is darkness already. Turns out that Ansel had a secret that he hadn't told anyone and was trying to block, but of course I heard it 'cause hearing thoughts and breaking through blocks are my specialties. Anyway, it was about a girl that he liked, but she didn't like him, and he embarrassed himself in front of her—you know—typical stuff. But that was enough unhappiness for him to be a target of the black hole or the energy vortex or whatever you want to call it.

The old me was enough for me to be the first target. Not the happiest of characters, was I? And when other students heard about what happened to us, some of them started to feel worried, too, and that opened the door for the darkness to come in to them.

Then Lance told us about Old Earth. I knew some of it from Past Class, but not everything. I know there is stuff Lance left out, too. I caught pictures in his mind of death camps in Germany and a tall building with a plane crashing into it called nine eleven for some reason. That's a strange name for a plane. Then he moved forward with his words, and I couldn't catch any more of his thoughts.

The idea was the same. Everything he told us about made people afraid. And when people are afraid you can control them. But the next part was what we came for. Who wants us afraid? And how can we stop them? That's what we're going to talk about tomorrow. We're meeting at two. It means skipping another class. I'll send Magnum a note.

I'm packing up now to go to Healing Pod for the night. That kid Jeori talked to me after Lance dismissed us, and he told me all about the massage and the whirlpool and the good sleep he and Ansel got. So why not??!! Maybe all of us will end up there—a real party!

~ Chapter 35 ~

Jeori and Ansel joyfully spent a second night in Healing Pod. All ten students who had been having frightening dreams or the uncomfortable feeling of being watched decided to join them. It really turned out to be quite a party. There were not enough massage therapists on evening duty for all of them, so Jeori and Ansel made do with the hot whirlpool and the steam room. Kad received the last massage of the night, and when he finally joined the younger students in the large communal tub, he began telling his most outrageous jokes. Jeori could hardly believe this was the same kid who had once seemed so unhappy. The laughter and the hot water did their work, and by lights out the entire group rolled into their beds warm, relaxed, and free from fear.

~ ~ ~

Wednesday dawned gray and dripping. Jeori awakened first. The room felt cold, and the boy pulled the fluffy comforter up around his shoulders as he stared out the window at the rain. He wondered what conclusions Lance and Lula had reached. But more, he wondered what they would be expected to do about it.

I've been thinking about the very same thing. Jeori turned to see Kadrun Black getting out of bed. *Thanks for suggesting this, Jeori,* Kad thought to him. *It's just what I needed. I've been feeling sort of guilty about bringing this down on us.*

Jeori smiled and shook his head. *Don't worry about it. If it wasn't you, it would have been somebody else. You know...I can hear your thoughts perfectly.*

Well yes, you seem to be hearing me just fine. This is new to you, huh?

Yeah, but you could read everyone's minds all along. Isn't that right, Kad?

The teenager smiled and walked over to Jeori, who sat up in bed. *You want to get dressed and have an early breakfast? I smell bacon!*

~ ~ ~

So began a new and unexpected friendship. Over breakfast and for an hour afterward until the other students began wandering in, Kad and Jeori talked and alternately popped thoughts back and forth between them. They joked and formed some outrageous notions of how to get rid of "The Beast" that was stalking them—from setting his underpants on fire, to breathing garlic in his face, to telling jokes so funny that he simply split apart, unable to stand the strain.

Kadrun discovered that Jeori was easy to talk to and a good listener. For the first time ever the teenager felt comfortable enough to talk about himself. He shared some of his old past and then told the younger boy about forming his new past. Jeori thought this new past stuff was simply brilliant.

~ Chapter 36 ~

The I.T. students were already seated when Professor Kartoofle staggered in. He looked terrible. His dark blonde hair was sticking out at odd angles. There were dark circles under both eyes, and his clothes were wrinkled. Kad looked over at Jeori and raised his eyebrows. A quiet thought passed between them. *He's had the dreams.*

"Sorry, class." Lance stifled a yawn. "It was a rough night, and now it is I who has a story to tell you. I was getting ready for today's meeting with you, and it was getting late. At two a.m. I finally put my head down on my desk for a moment's rest. I fell fast asleep.

"Suddenly I found myself in a forest. It was nighttime. Glowing eyes were circling me in the dark. And yes...I could smell pine trees. That was the only good part of the dream. The eyes kept drawing closer, and I looked frantically around trying to find a way out of the center of their circle. But it was hopeless. I suddenly realized that I was in a dream and did what I've always done to wake up...I looked down at my hand. Usually shifting my attention to my hand will awaken me...but not this time.

"This dream morphed into others, all frightening, all concerning eyes and being trapped or spied upon. I finally awakened at dawn still slumped over my desk. I climbed into bed fully clothed to get a little more sleep and just woke up a little while ago. And here I am... looking my very best for you." He laughed weakly at his own joke.

"Okay...let's all take a deep breath." Lance took one himself, and the students followed. "Before I fell asleep I spent much of last evening on conference calls with Lula and other I.T. teachers around the globe. Yes, in answer to your thoughts, this phenomenon is indeed starting to happen with dem poppers everywhere. People of every age, but especially young people, are beginning to encounter this smelly black hole."

There was a chuckle from the back of the classroom, and then another from the front. Then the whole class was laughing. "What did I say?" their teacher asked shaking his tired head in confusion.

Jake spoke up. "You said (and the entire class joined in) *smelly black hole!*"

"Oh...I did, didn't I? Ha-ha!"

Laughter erupted again. After a minute, the hilarity died down to the occasional chuckle. "I'm glad you all remember how to laugh," Lance said, finally able to put on a serious face. "Laughter is good medicine.

"So...let's continue. As we spoke of yesterday, Old Earth was full of fear and distrust. Fears were used and sometimes *created* by politicians, religious leaders, and business leaders to gain power and that stuff called money that people thought was so important back then.

"But just a few decades ago what happened? Yes... Allicia?"

"People stopped being afraid."

"You're absolutely right! People suddenly realized how alike they were. They began to feel each other's feelings, each other's hopes, and each other's dreams for the future which were so like their own. As age old fears and distrust dissolved, there was a burst of freedom felt all over the world.

"Then gradually people began to hear each other's thoughts. We're still in the formative stages of that process. You know all this. You know how speaking mind to mind brings you closer to your neighbors. You know that without money or individually owned stuff, there can be no greed and no stealing. You know when there is no lack, and when you have choices of what you want to study and where you want to live, joy and creativity happen. Think of all the discoveries since the change; force field technology, cold fusion for energy production, advanced robotics, new building materials and methods, natural ways of healing the human body, new methods of cleaning up our planet with advances in solar and wind technology, even use of a special type of bacterium which cleans up nuclear waste...and oh yes, interdimensional travel. So with all this going on, with all this excitement and with new discoveries being made almost on a daily basis, why would anybody on Earth want to take us back into the dark times?"

Kadrun slowly raised his hand. "Maybe it's nobody *on Earth*."

Lance nodded. "Yes, Kad, I think you may be right." Suppose for just a minute that there are sentient beings from another planet who are messing with us, trying to gain...or perhaps regain control over Earth's population. Suppose that the fears built up over the centuries and many of the terrible things that happened on Old Earth were actually instigated from the outside?"

The students began turning around in their seats and whispering excitedly to their neighbors. "You all sound like a bunch of owls," their teacher began, "Who-o-o, who-o-o, who-o-o!" Everyone laughed...

and again, the laughter felt good. Lance raised his hand. The class grew quiet.

"It was my new friend Lula who discovered the first reference in a book written near the end of the last century. This book and several other sources we later discovered described beings who had come to Earth from another planet...beings who were so into using their brains that they had lost all else. Hope, love, compassion, and humor were unknown to them. All they had left was the desire for power. Long, long ago these aliens first targeted the Earth. They got into ancient people's minds to create distrust and fear and then violence. They changed people's memories and found ways to cancel the natural abilities that we are now regaining. There was even the suggestion that they actually changed Earth's written history to fit their needs for control. Oh, they were dark characters, indeed!

"So here we come into this new day, a day they actually helped create by pushing fear to such an extreme. You see, eventually everyone everywhere came to a point where the amount of fear mongering got so ridiculous that they said no...no to the craziness, no to being manipulated, no to fear being pushed in their faces over and over and over again. I must say that my dreams last night have also done what I'm sure was not anticipated or desired by those who sent them. I feel more confident than ever that we can and will put a stop to this!"

Kad interrupted. "But you still haven't answered our question, Lance. Who is causing all of this?" They're not from Earth, okay...but who are they? Is there some reason you don't want us to know?"

"There is the old notion that if you name something you draw it to you, Kad. But other beliefs claim just the opposite, that if you learn the name of something you gain power over it. I don't personally subscribe to either notion, but we shall see what we shall see.

"Our research led us past an alien species known as the *Grays* which seemed less likely, to a reptilian species called the *Anunnaki*. We felt as if we'd hit gold when we stumbled on this group." Lance barked out a laugh and shook his head.

Jeori glanced at Kadrun, and they shared a thought. *What's so funny about that?*

"Now, the Anunnaki were described as walking on two legs, sort of like your cat people, Ansel, but unlike the cat people they are neither kind nor wise. Their heads are shaped like lizards' heads and they are scaled with long flexible tails. Strangely, Lula and I uncovered vids of a television series made over fifty years ago. It involved a race of alien lizards disguised as humans who were trying to take over the Earth. But of course no one took this seriously.

Delving deeper we found a source which claimed that the Anunnaki experimented on early humans, changing their genetic structure and turning them into frightened, well-controlled slaves to mine gold which the aliens wanted to send back to their home planet.

"Do any of you like to read the old legends of Earth?" More than half of the students raised their hands. "Good! So I'm asking you. Does this remind you of anything...anything at all?" There was a moment of silence....Yes, Jeori?"

"I know! I know! Dragons! It reminds me of dragons, Lance! And in the old stories dragons coveted gold, too! Oh...and there was something about dragon eyes. If you stared into a dragon's eyes then...then...." Jeori shivered and couldn't go on.

2065

The class sat in stunned silence as they took this in. Could it be? Is that where the stories of dragons came from...from a *memory*...of *aliens*?

~ ~ ~

Lance shook his head. "I know it's a lot to take in. Now, let's take a few moments to breathe and ground our energy, and then we...."

"Look! There on the wall!" Sonia pointed to a place near the door. "They must have a spy or something. See that small black spot? It feels wrong...and it wasn't there before. I'm sure of it!" All eyes turned to where the girl pointed.

Professor Kartoofle rose and started moving slowly toward the back of the room. Yes, he saw it, too. It could almost be a fly on the wall...almost.

"Come, Leemon!" Lance said in a demanding tone. Students gasped as a red-tailed hawk shivered into sight beside their teacher. It hopped up onto Allicia's desk. The girl moved back to give the large bird room. It fluffed its wings. Lance ran his hand gently over the bird's head and down his feathered back. "Let's see what we have here, my friend." He held out his arm, and the hawk climbed on. Man and hawk moved resolutely toward the back wall, both watching the dark spot intently as they drew closer and closer and closer.

"....Careful, Lance!" Jeori warned.

Quick as lightning, Leemon reached out and pecked at the wall with his sharp beak.

The dark spot was gone.

~ Chapter 37 ~

Professor Kartoofle turned around and walked slowly back up the center aisle of his classroom. As he reached the front of the class he turned, and the large hawk disappeared from his arm.

"How many of you could see Leemon clearly?" Lance asked, looking around. "I hoped that the sending would be strong, but I couldn't tell if all of you could make him out."

Every hand but three rose into the air. "This is very fine. Those of you who didn't see him this time should not be concerned. Clairvoyance is much like gaining telepathy or teleporting or traveling interdimensionally. It is a matter of practice and playing in your imagination. You three did feel his energy, though?" The three nodded.

"Did your bird eat the dark spot, Lance?" Michiko asked. "I couldn't see from my angle."

"I don't think so. I feel my fine friend confused the *spy* as you put it. It looked as if it disappeared the moment he struck at it."

"And this suggests something! Have any of you heard the term *totem animal?*"

Kad nodded and slowly raised his hand.

"Is that what Leemon is...a totem animal?" Jake asked, running a hand through his curly black hair.

"Yes, Jake. My hawk and I have been friends for many years. The truth is that he is a part of me. He is the part of me that is clear-eyed and strong and fearless. He is also a wonderful messenger. I call on him when I want to remember my own courage, or when I want to send or receive a message using my deeper senses.

"I'm thinking that this might be just the time for each of you to choose your own totem animal. If this worked so well on our spy, think what we might do with a roomful of animals! What do you think?" There were excited nods all around the room.

"Does it need to be something fierce, Lance?" Thomas asked.

"Your totem can be any kind of animal you like. But as you choose it, it will also be choosing you. I suggest going with the first animal that shows up in your imagination. If it doesn't seem to suit you, you may ask it to change to something else.

"All right, let's begin. First take a deep cleansing breath, in through your nose and out through your mouth. Continue breathing in this way a few times as you relax.... Good! Now go to your sanctuary, your favorite imagined place, whether it's in a garden or in a forest or on a mountain top or by the seashore. Raise your hand when you're there.... Good! Now feel all the happiness of being in your sanctuary.... Oh, this is going very smoothly. You are all such good imaginers.

"Now as you relax in this most special place that is yours alone, an animal is coming to greet you. See what comes. It will stop right in front of you and stare into your eyes. Do you see it? Raise your hand when you do.... Good. Now reach out and touch your animal. Pay attention to how it makes you feel. Does it fill you with joy? When you feel a clear connection with your new animal helper, raise your hand again.... Good. Now open your eyes. That's all there is to it!"

The students spent the next half hour describing their totems and what had happened at first contact. There was a flying squirrel—clever and quick, a fiercely protective grizzly bear, a shiny black raven, a wise-eyed cougar, a sharp-beaked bald eagle, a long and sinuous python, and a massive striped tiger. There was a spotted leopard—and another leopard, dark as midnight, a large grey wolf, an elephant with long tusks, and an agile dolphin leaping the waves. The descriptions continued until each student had taken a turn.

"Good work, everyone!" Lance concluded. "Now, each of you can call on your totem animal, this special friend of yours, at any time. It will watch over you when you sleep. It will come in to warn you if any suspicious or out of the ordinary energies are near you. You can also send it out on errands to bring back information for you. The answers will appear in your minds.

"I'd like you to each practice connecting with your totem until our next meeting. See if it will give you a name it would like to be called. Or you may make one up that seems right. I suspect that having your new friend with you will help you feel safer and more protected.

"Remember what happened today with my totem. The beings sending that dark spot on the wall—let's call them Anunnaki—didn't like being confronted with a power they couldn't understand. Think about the other powers you possess that they don't. We will take it from here next regular class period. Kadrun, please join us if you're able. You were the first, and I feel you may already have the answer we are seeking."

Kad looked up in surprise.

2065

~ ~ ~

Late again! The slim girl with the spiky, white-blond hair was hurrying toward Advanced Teleportation which was third door down from Interdimensional Travel. In her rush she paid no attention when a tall teenage boy wearing a white, hooded sweatshirt and blue jeans passed her in the hall. It wasn't until a few moments later that the logo on his sweatshirt and his softly spoken words came back to her. What he had said was "Hullo, Elf."

Cleo turned around. But it was too late. Kad was gone.

~ Chapter 38 ~

Kad's Diary

Thursday

Hi diary, Kadrun Black here! I have my new totem animal lying on the floor beside me. He—no, she—is a beautiful shiny black leopard. I'll get her name soon.... It's close to coming in.

It's funny that I knew anything about animal totems. The other older new kid, Carlos, who's in Life as a Play with me, was talking about totems at lunch just last week. He learned about them in the pod where he was before this. His old pod was called Cultural Anthropology, and they study how people lived in different parts of the world. He told me he's got this clever chimpanzee named Harley that follows him everywhere and helps him to remember to laugh and have fun. He said he used to be shy. I said I think lots of kids who choose Actors' Pod used to be something else.

I like my leopard because she is sure of herself and strong...and black of course. She is like a part of me I forgot. She fits me. She is like the protective mother I wish I'd had and the strong part of me all rolled into one.

Oh ...and I ran into Cleo on my way out of I.T. today. I said hello, but I guess she didn't hear me.

Now I've got to get to this assignment for Mz. Lipton. I missed her last class, and we were supposed to have the outline of our play done. I'll stick it under her door with a note. Yeah, here it comes. I'll do the beekeeper in space idea, but I'll make the beekeeper an ex model from Fiber Arts named...yeah, Ippsy Bobbinsford! This won't take any time at all. Two acts I can do. So here goes.

2065

Assignment for Beginning Playwriting
Kadrun Black 10/23/2065

Scene 1: Inside of an old beat up space ship. Main cabin has four boxes full of bees. You can see tall flowers growing in raised area [stage right] for the bees. Several jerky robots in silver suits are watering the flowers with old fashioned watering cans.

Narrator introduces Ippsy Bobbinsford. Her story...turned away by the only man she ever loved...blah, blah, blah...She decides to go into outer space and chooses this old barge called the Honey Bee because her nickname is Honey and her last name starts with B....Honey Bee. So she thinks it's a sign. She trades all her credits...blah, blah, blah...What she doesn't realize is that the old spaceship is really a production center for making honey...with real live bees! By the time she understands, it's too late to back out.

The new ship's captain, Honey Bobbinsford enters stage left. She is tall and honey blonde, dolled up, wearing her tight silver spacesuit and high heels.

Honey checks on the bees. Then she stands in front of the mirror trying out a few hairstyles. She is so bored. She talks to the bees and then to herself and out of her mouth come the most outrageous puns. She has no idea of what she is saying. She pulls her hair up and pins it into a hair style called a Beehive. [Goes off stage briefly comes back wearing wig.] Honey thinks she looks great and spins around accidentally knocking down one of the bee boxes. The bees go crazy and swarm around, finally landing in her Beehive hairdo where they settle down for the night.

Ippsy tries to sleep sitting up. She wakes up tired and crabby with bees swarming around her head. Angry, she finally grabs the deserted bee box off the ground where it fell and slams it onto her head. The bees leave her hair for whatever is left of the honeycomb inside the bee box. She removes the bee box from her beehive which is ruined and sticky with honey.

Scene 2: Inside of the Mars space station. Ippsy enters stage left. She has two jars of honey in her hands to drop off. Her ship docked before she got a chance to clean herself up, and she's a dripping, gooey mess.

 Enter stage right Kadrun Black, Ippsy's long lost love. He has been searching for her all over space...apologies and more silly puns and declarations of love. Honey, you're bee-witching and bee-u-ti-ful. You bee-dazzle me by just bee-ing you...bee mine... yuck, yuck. Several left over bees fly out of Honey's beehive and sting Kadrun on the nose. He stamps his feet and spins around in a crazy way. Ippsy grabs him, thinking he is dancing, and they dance around together. The end! [This will be a musical later. I will play Ippsy. Someone else will play me.]

~ Chapter 39 ~

By the time Professor Kartoofle shuffled into class on Friday afternoon, Kadrun Black had a good portion of the students in Interdimensional Travel laughing their heads off. Jeori was amazed that anyone could remember so many jokes.

As all eyes fell on Lance, the room grew still. The teacher yawned as he reached his desk and pulled himself into his chair. "I think this has gone on quite long enough," he said, stifling yet another yawn. Jeori and Kadrun shared a look.

"Did you have more bad dreams?" Michiko asked. "Scary ones?" added Sonia.

Lance nodded and rubbed a finger across one eyelid. "Again last night I stayed up too late looking over my notes. As it got later, I found myself becoming more and more concerned over everything that's been happening. And I was so tired from lack of sleep the night before that I stupidly forgot to call on Leemon to accompany me in my dreams. We don't get help unless we ask for it...right?

"This time a dark cloud was chasing me across a green meadow. It was a huge, angry, rolling thing. I could feel the coldness of it as the wind it produced pushed against my back. I glanced up behind me at the sky. It was gaining on me! I felt afraid but also tired and hopeless. It seemed as if I was running through quicksand, with each step harder to take than the one before. Finally I stumbled, and the darkness fell on me. I couldn't see out of it. I was trapped! I felt weak and afraid and so sorry for myself. I was about to give up. But as I lay there, my mind drifted to all the good times I've had. And suddenly I felt sorry for that cloud instead. Just like that the darkness disappeared.

"Now, let's all take a few deep and cleansing breaths. This will give us what we need right now... more energy and clarity. We can't be worrying about the past or about the future while we're concentrating on our breathing. Now is our point of power. Well, look at that! I see that our visiting comedian has the solution shining around him. Would you care to share it, Kadrun?"

Kad shook his head. "I have no idea what you're talking about."

"Sorry to put you on the spot here, Kad. Is it or is it not true that recently you have created a new motto for yourself?" The teenager nodded.

"It is just three words that blaze around him like a beacon. Perhaps some of you can sense this. Kadrun, would you mind sharing your new motto with the class?"

"I didn't know I was being that obvious. But okay. My new motto is *Do the Unexpected*. Is that what you mean?"

"Yes, exactly. Do the unexpected. Now to review... what made fear and hatred finally stop on Earth?"

"People let go of the dark feelings," Jake answered.

"That's right, Jake. Instead of doing what the negative energies wanted and expected, which was for people to feel fear and anger and guilt, all people on Earth began to walk away from what they didn't want and towards what they did. You see what happened in my dream."

"You mean we're supposed to *love* the darkness?' Ansel asked, wrinkling his upper lip in disgust. "It tried to hurt me. That makes me feel angry."

"Indeed. But listen to what you just said, Ansel. It *makes* you feel angry. If you want to feed dark energies you can't do better than that. One of my favorite sayings is from a very wise woman who lived long ago. It is this: *What you resist persists.* If you push against something you give it more power to push you right back."

"So we're supposed to just allow it?"

"There's no 'supposed to' here, Ansel. There is only what works and what doesn't work. Fear left the world because first people made a decision to turn toward a better way of feeling. Then they followed up with action. We have the same choice now. And look at it this way. We live now in a way that works well for Earth's people. So all these desperate beings can do is to try to create fear, basically out of nothing. If we don't fear, but instead feel strong in what we are...if when we encounter the darkness we send the feeling of love and compassion instead...."

"And maybe even laugh?" Kadrun added, nodding his head.

"Yes, that's an excellent idea, Kad. Remember that in the description Lula found, the aliens didn't understand humor. So laughter should confuse them greatly."

"But Lance," Ansel asked with a hint of anger in his voice, "are you saying that we just forget what they've done and pretend that it doesn't matter?"

"Does it really matter...unless we allow it to?"

There was a long silence. "I think I get it," Ansel said finally. "By getting all angry we give away our power...just like we do by fearing the darkness. And that's what they want."

"...Exactly!" Remember, no matter who they are or where they come from, without our participation, they've got nothing. So what do you think, class? Shall we go out hunting?"

Kad's Diary

Friday

As soon as Lance said the words, I had the feeling that this hunting idea wouldn't work. Everyone but me was sort of scared but really more excited. The mood was all wrong. Dark energies can only mess with people when they are tired or sad or angry or worried. But I didn't say anything. Now that's the usual old Kad.

So we lay down on the soft blue rug at the front of the room. Then we went into our trance states and traveled out in ten minute segments searching different dimensions and planets. Lance stayed back to watch over us and call us out and question us afterward. We did this three times. We went everywhere we could think of—anywhere we'd ever been. It was a big fat zero—no evil eye, no black hole, no forest smell—nothing.

Then I had to open my big mouth. I told the class that what we needed was a real good actor to pretend at being unhappy and tired so that the black hole would come. Everyone turned and stared at me.... I walked right into that one, right?

I said I could do it. (I sure hope I can.) So Lance told me to stay after class and............

I'm downstairs now. Glory (my leopard) put her paw on my knee. I'd told her to warn me if any weird energy came around—and she did. Just then the scary feeling started. Something was in my room! I grabbed my journal and left. The aliens must think I'm the perfect target. That's actually

2065

good for what we intend to do. But Lance and I have to be ready so we can do this together, me to do it and him to watch and listen and call me out.

So I'm in the cafeteria sitting in the middle where it's crowded. I ran into Phoebe on the way down and asked her to scan energies for me and tell me if anything starts to feel wrong. She is at the next table over, watching me. She doesn't know what this is all about. I will tell her after.

So... here it is. After class Lance said he knew it was parents' weekend. I told him no parents, no problem. He said he had some free time. So this is the plan. Tomorrow at four I'll be in my room. I'll open my comp so he can hear me and I can hear him. Then I'll put excitement away and take on depression and worry. Lots of practice on that! When the negative energy starts I'll go all pathetic and say "Who are you? Leave me alone!" Then I'll stagger to my bed. That will signal Lance, and he'll time me for fifteen minutes. He said ten. I said fifteen. We'll see if I can switch from fear to sending loving energies, humor—whatever it takes to make the darkness disappear. I'll come back when either the dark energy is gone or when Lance says the code word... whichever comes first. Then he'll walk across to Actors' Pod and up to my room to make sure I'm okay. This should be interesting....

~ Chapter 40 ~

Professor Kartoofle blew out his breath and checked the time again. It was seventeen minutes past four. Not a peep or a groan out of Kadrun yet. The young actor had promised to put on worry and then his most weak and frightened manner as soon as he felt the energy in his room shift. What was taking so long?

There! It was beginning. Lance began timing. He smiled. Kad was really getting into it moving out from their decided upon script. Now he was pleading. Now he was moaning softly.

Even though he was across the quad, when the quiet finally came Lance could feel the deep and forbidding darkness that surrounded Kad. He listened closely now...nothing. He didn't expect to hear anything, but still.... Lance shivered.

The huge Red Tail flew in through the wall and landed. "Leemon," Lance breathed. "What?" Then he felt it. *Oh no! Not here!* He lowered his computer screen, took a deep breath, and looked behind him. Yes! There on the wall! That dark spot!

Taking another breath the young man forced out a laugh. "It's so nice to see you, old chum. What brings you here?" Lance cocked his head quickly toward the back of the room and sent a silent message to his totem. Leemon turned and savagely struck with his curved beak. The spy was gone.

~ ~ ~

Kadrun groaned and was quiet. He was moving down a long tunnel, the dim light behind him gradually fading to total darkness. He inched forward. There was no good aroma of pine trees to greet him this time. Instead, a smell of rot and decay began to burn his nose and throat. It got stronger the farther he went.

Kad felt movement at his back. Something was sneaking up behind him! He turned blindly and reached back. His hand touched a wet wall. *This isn't real,* he thought.

The fifteen-year-old slowly ghosted forward again. The tunnel walls were pushing in from both sides now. Kad could barely squeeze through the narrowed channel. A few steps more, and he was forced to stop. One wall was at his back and another directly in front of him. The walls felt slimy and gluey, and in moments they moved in to surround him more tightly. They seemed alive. He felt...yes...as if he was being swallowed. *This isn't real,* he tried again. Fear galloped up to meet him.

Kad tried to take a breath. He tried to remember his mission. Make a joke! Yes, laugh! But he couldn't think clearly enough to find a joke. Yes, *compassion.* That was the word, but his thoughts were muddy. What did that word mean exactly? The walls pushed at him.

A thought came.... *I feel like laundry bumping around in a washing machine.* Kadrun chuckled. *Yes!* "You're so cute!" he said as laughter burst from his throat. "I must taste quite delicious...yum-yum!" Kad knew he wasn't making sense, but he was way past caring. The movement around him paused as if whatever causing it was confused. "Oh, yes...a washing machine! I will come out *so* clean and fresh. Do you have a proper dryer or will I be allowed to air dry?" Just in time his recently discovered sense of humor was rushing in. "Have you heard the one about the wide-mouthed frog?"

Yes! The movement of the walls had stopped. The darkness seemed to be shifting attention—as if waiting for something. "I can wait too, you know. *I am* Kadrun Black. I have waited before."

There! Something had shifted. He was now looking from the darkness into a familiar room. It was his room in the old house on Maple Street. It still held his wooden crib...and the pale blue rocking chair that his mother had never used.

Kad watched as the young Doreen carried the squalling baby through the bedroom door to the changing table. She began to change the baby's diapers. She worked quickly and a bit roughly. The baby cried.

Kad understood what was happening. The aliens were trying to use his past to defeat him. He could sense them watching, as he in turn watched the scene they had picked up from his early life. Kad watched his mother carefully.

Doreen lifted the baby from the changing table and stiffly carried him to his crib. She put him down, efficiently tucked the blue blanket around him, turned off the table lamp, and started to leave the room. The young woman turned back, the light from the hallway putting her in shadow. "Nothing happened the way it was supposed to." The shadow shook its head. "I should never have had you. It's not your fault, baby. I don't know how to love you." The doorway stood empty.

The image faded. A tear rolled down Kadrun's cheek. "You only wanted the one love you couldn't have," he whispered as darkness surrounded him once more. "But I was there for you...if you'd ever bothered to pay attention," he added as the old feelings of anger and betrayal hit him for the thousandth time. He choked out a sob. "Was I such an ugly baby, Doreen?" "Did I cry too much for you to even *try* to love me?" The walls were nudging him again. Oh yes, they liked *that*.

Feeding time, the teenager thought. But that one thought stopped him cold. Was this really the way he wanted it to end? He slowly replayed the scene in his mind. His mother felt helpless and angry and denied the life she'd wanted, so she refused to enjoy the life she already had. *Just like me,* he suddenly realized. *I felt that very same way for all those years before I joined Actors' Pod.* The teenager shut his eyes tight then reopened them in the darkness. He drew in a ragged breath. The hungry dark pushed against him eagerly and squeezed tighter, ready to feed on his life force.

But Kad had made his decision. He was past feeling panic or even anger. "No...no, you don't win," he said softly. "I won't give you what you want."

Kadrun's thoughts turned to his mother. "Doreen Connelly, I finally understand how alike we were," Kadrun said into the stale air. "We both wasted so much time wanting the one love we couldn't have, didn't we?" He took another breath. "If I can accept everything about myself and move on, then I have to be able to accept you, too. I can let you be yourself, and I can stop hurting myself over something I can never have. I hope you finally found a way to be happy."

Kadrun Connelly Black took a deep breath as a beam of warm energy burst through his heart then spread throughout his body. Compassion had come at last.

Was the darkness less? Yes! The walls were pulling back, and the tunnel was lighter. Kad realized that he was actually seeing *through* the light. This could mean only one thing—that the light was coming from him.

The teenager looked around himself. "You aliens or dark forces or whatever it is that you are...do you know what? You helped me to understand. Thank you for showing me the choice I had to make. You may not be able to comprehend this, but right now I even feel compassion for you. You don't know how to laugh. You don't know how to love or care. You have so little, and so you try to steal power from people by convincing us to feel hurt and angry and afraid and guilty." He took another breath. It seemed easier this time. The bad smell was dissipating. "We on Earth have chosen to live in a better way now...in a happier way. Just as I feel compassion for you, so will the others you try to control. You can turn away from me now," Kad said in a strong, clear voice. "There is nothing left for you here."

With a jerk the fifteen-year-old re-entered his body and opened his eyes. He was in his own room again stretched out on his single bed. The darkness was gone. But the feeling of love, the feeling of being whole that he had discovered in and through that darkness, it had stayed. It bathed Kad like sunlight, and he basked in the new freedom he felt. Tears of relief rolled down his cheeks. "My old past is finally healed," he whispered...and meant it.

~ ~ ~

"Elephant ears!" said a clear and familiar voice. There was a moment of silence. Then all that could be heard through the link was wild and crazy laughter.

"Oh, no...oh, no...Kad, are you all right?" There was more laughter.

"*Elephant ears? What kind of a code is that?*" Kadrun barked. "No, I'm not all right, Lance! I'm way better than all right!"

Relief was obvious in Lance's voice as he spoke again. "I'll be right over."

"No need," Kad replied. "I'll meet you in the Art Pod cafeteria in five minutes. I need to get some fresh air, anyway. That tunnel stinks."

~ Chapter 41 ~

Kadrun Black practically bounced out the door and down the path toward his old pod. He slowed when he noticed his friend Jeori talking with an older couple up ahead.

"Hi, Jeori," the teenager said as he approached. "And this must be your mom and dad. I'm Kadrun Black...a new friend of Jeori's," he said, shaking their hands. "I hope you know you raised a really good kid here. Sorry that I can't stay longer. Professor Kartoofle is waiting for me in the cafeteria." He looked meaningfully at Jeori.

Jeori's eyes widened. "You look different, Kad. Your energy is all golden and kind of sparkly. Did you...?"

"*I did*, Jeori. It's over. We'll talk soon." With a quick wave he was off.

~ ~ ~

The teenager, who had always seemed so serious, was actually grinning as he walked through the main Art Pod doors. Kadrun Connelly Black had never felt so good in all his life. Even when he had decided to become the "new Kad" there were still some hurts that he hadn't been able to totally dissolve, some old secrets that he had still kept carefully guarded. But at this moment...!

He took a deep breath and looked around. Art Pod wasn't looking so bad to him now. The colors were brighter than he remembered. The energies of everyone he passed were the happy, creative energies of artists on the move.

His smile was still in place when he unexpectedly came toe to toe with Cleopatra Murphy who was just leaving the cafeteria. "There you are, Elf!" Kad exclaimed. Without thinking he picked her up and twirled her around.

"Whoa! What's gotten into you?" Kadrun laughed as he put her down, and Cleo thought she had never heard a more beautiful sound. "You look...you look... well, actually...*happy.*"

"It's freedom, Cleo. That's what it is. I'm finally, finally free! I've got to meet professor Kartoofle right now, but if you have any time tomorrow, maybe we could...."

"Yes!" Cleo answered without waiting for him to finish. "Tomorrow would be perfect."

As he entered the Art Pod cafeteria, Kadrun spotted Lance Kartoofle immediately. The Interdimensional Travel teacher had cleverly positioned himself for privacy at the end of a table near the back corner of the room. A handful of students were either talking together or visiting with their parents at tables closer to the door, but the area near Lance was empty.

Kad waved his hand and headed right over. He could hardly wait to share his story with Lance. He had done it! He Kadrun Black had met and vanquished the darkness!

So for nearly the first time in his life Kad forgot his usual caution. He forgot to block his thoughts and emotions. Some of the students he passed stopped what they were doing and turned to stare at him. Not all of the students were telepathic, but enough.

Kad sat down across from his old teacher, and with great excitement he told the tale of what had happened to him in the tunnel. Then for nearly an hour afterward he and Lance formed a strategy for what would come next. The I.T. teacher had of course put up a block of white noise so no one could pick up their conversation. But it was already too late. The damage had been done.

~ ~ ~

The explosion happened the next morning. Rumors were flying everywhere, morphing into other rumors, becoming bigger with every telling.

It was eleven-thirty Sunday morning, the exact time Kadrun Black had agreed to meet Cleo Murphy. Stares and whispers followed him as he stepped through the door of the Art Pod Lounge and pulled back the hood on his white sweatshirt.

Elf, he thought as he noticed her.

Cleo rolled her eyes. *Outside*, she thought back.

Kad turned on his heels, and Cleo rose and followed him out. Several students stood up as if to do the same.

The teenager stuck his head back in the door. "Sit! Stay!" he barked. A few chuckles of embarrassment followed Kadrun as he left the lounge for the second time.

The two made their way quickly through a press of students, out the main Art Pod door, and into the fresh air and sunshine. Kad grabbed Cleo's hand, and they took off running. Laughing, they sprinted through the center of the quad between Actors' Pod and Fiber Arts and out into the meadow beyond.

Kadrun led Cleo to a large tree with leafy branches hanging to the ground. They stepped inside the green and golden leafed room. A waterproof camping blanket had been carefully laid out on fallen leaves. "You planned this?" Cleo asked, looking around.

"....Yup! I've got a story to tell you, and I thought some privacy would be good. Nice, isn't it? And there's more." Kad flourished his arm like a magician and pulled a large paper bag out of his Actors' Guild backpack. "I stopped in the kitchen and got us lunch." He produced two bottles of flavored water, two oranges, and a sandwich for each of them.

"This is about the biggest sandwich I've ever seen," Cleo said as she carefully pulled back the paper on her fully loaded pastrami sub. "How did you manage it?"

"I told Cyndi that I was eating outside, and that I could sure use two sandwiches since I was really hungry. This is what she made me."

"You mean Cyndi from Cuisine Arts...Cyndi with the dimples and the long black hair?" Kad nodded. "She rotates with our pod, too. She must really like you."

Kad shrugged. "Maybe," he answered and took a bite.

As they ate their lunch Kad told his story. Cleo listened with rapt attention. He began with his first experience with the dark during Interdimensional Travel Class; the smell of pine trees, spotting the black hole, being swallowed by the dark tunnel, and Lance bringing him out. Then he moved into everything that had happened since, including the strange dreams and the feeling of being watched that people were beginning to experience—not only in their quad, but in quads all over the world. He left nothing out of his telling, even explaining to Cleo the vision of his mother and how that had forced him into the choice... find compassion and survive or stay angry and be destroyed. He'd thought it would be hard to tell her that part. But strangely—looking into her green eyes, it wasn't hard at all.

"Lance is planning a big assembly for tomorrow morning for everyone in Art Pod," Kad said taking a bite of his sandwich. "He'll give an overview of what's been happening—including his trip to Central Division Library and what he discovered there. Then I'll tell my story—well most of it, anyway. I'll leave out the specific stuff about my mother. No need to cause any more grief. This will be shot in vid and played for the rest of the quad. Then Lance asked if I would like to help edit the vid with any do-overs I want...and then guess what, Elf?"

"What?" she asked, finishing half of the sandwich and wrapping the rest for later.

"The vid will be sent to quads all over the world so that these aliens or dark forces can be defeated once and for all!"

"Wow! That's really something, Kad. You'll be helping to save the whole world. Are you scared about so many people seeing you?"

"No, I'm excited, Elf. This is my big break into acting! I hope you don't mind that I practiced on you." He smiled.

"Silly," she said. "I'm glad I'm the one you wanted to practice with."

"Cleo, you've got something on your mouth."

"I do?" She began to reach up to her lips.

"No...here, let me do it." Kad leaned over...and kissed her.

Cleo giggled. "You're sneaky."

Kad laughed. "Yup," he said...and kissed her again.

~ Chapter 42 ~

As far away as a space station on the edge of the Milky Way and as near as the blink of an eye, the aliens watched, confused by love they could not know and by laughter they would never understand. But one emotion they knew well. And that was anger.

~ ~ ~

"What? What was that?" Cleo began to swivel her head to look behind her.

Kad gently placed a hand on each of her cheeks and turned her head to face him again. "It was nothing, Elf," he said as he kissed her for a third time. "No... no, it was nothing at all."

~ ~ ~

The Anunnaki counsel watched in stony silence. Slowly Grand Leader turned to address the gathered Assembly of the One Hundred. "From current projections I must conclude that it is pointless to waste any more effort on this puny planet," he announced in his cold voice. "We leave for Vega One immediately. Vega has a humanoid species which is just becoming sentient. My calculations indicate that with proper manipulation we can expect a run of power as long and as successful as we have experienced on Earth."

Around the open portal scaly heads nodded. Then the low chanting began. "Vega One...Vega One...Vega One...Vega One...."

Grand Leader raised his hand for silence. "All may not be lost on this planet, however. As we all know, Earthlings are a fickle bunch. This peace and love nonsense cannot last forever. We will time our return for two hundred years from this day. By then humans will have forgotten our existence, and we will try again."

"Try again...try again...try again...." chanted the hundred.

~ Chapter 43 ~

Jeori Kellogg reached a hand out to sense the energy as his father, who was standing ten feet away, started to dissolve around the edges and then disappeared completely. "Bye, Dad," Jeori said into the space where his father had been the moment before.

"You need to be a bit more careful there, Jeori," his mother cautioned. "You don't want your energy field mixing with someone else's when they teleport. It could be dangerous for both of you. I've told you about this."

"I know, Mom. I just want to do it so bad. It can't be that hard...can it?"

"Hard no, but training first! I know it is difficult for an eleven-year-old to wait. I really do understand, but thirteen will come soon enough."

Jeori pouted. "Not for me."

"Want to escort me back to my quad? The walk might do you good."

"No thanks, Mom. I've got to see Kad and find out what happened."

"Ah, the big secret, is it? Okay, but remember what I said. Teleporting without training is definitely not an option."

"Yeah, I heard you...but I don't have to like it."

Jeori turned slowly and moved back toward his quad. His mom had said training, right? Kad would know how. They'd never talked about it, but Kad was fifteen. He must have teleported successfully by now. *Maybe he'll teach me.*

Jeori stopped and called in his mind. *Kadrun Black! This is your friend Jeori Kellogg calling. Can you hear me?*

There was no response coming back into his mind. He tried again. *Kad, can you hear me? Please answer.* He sighed. *Just one more stupid thing I don't know how to do,* he thought and kicked the grass in frustration.

Jeori walked by the main gallery and onto the new path holding the mosaic stepping stones that Kayla and her classmates had recently completed. He began hopping from one stone to the next. There, down the row of stones, was Kayla's sunny yellow flower surrounded by blue sky and the little white cloud. Jeori stopped when he came to it, and a smile crept to his face. Just seeing his best friend's creation made him feel better.

Someone stopped in front of him. He looked up.

"You called?"

"I did," Jeori said in wonder. You really heard me, Kad?"

"I really did. I'd just gotten back to my room. Ready to hear what happened?"

"Sure I am!" Jeori replied. "Follow me! I know just the place." They made their way past the spot where Jeori's dad had just disappeared and on to the other side of the field where tall grasses grew. "Now all we do is sit down right here! This grass is kinda wet, but I don't care if you don't. It should hide us real good."

They got settled. Then for the third time in two days Kadrun Black told his tale. When he was done....

"That's the most amazing story I've ever heard in my *whole entire life!*" Jeori gushed. "It should be a movie, just like the old movies from the before time. Wow! I would sure like to see a movie like that with all the darkness and all the scariness and you being the hero at the end. Heck, I'd like to make a movie like that. Wouldn't you, Kad?"

"Maybe," Kadrun answered. A small smile crept to the corners of his mouth. *This is what it's like to have friends,* he mused, keeping this thought strictly to himself.

So it was on this exciting day of secrets and stories that Jeori Kellogg forgot all about his driving desire to teleport and about the frustration of being eleven years old instead of thirteen.

~ ~ ~

And before he knew it, Jeori Kellogg *was* thirteen and already stretching out toward the tall man he would one day become.

At the end of his very first day of Teleportation I class, Jeori surprised his teacher by brilliantly porting patterns back and forth across the field—appearing here, disappearing, appearing there, and disappearing again. He simply couldn't contain himself! Mz. Landon proclaimed him the fastest learner she'd ever had the pleasure to teach! Then a strange look came over her face followed by narrowed eyes and a mask of suspicion.

Jeori blushed. Had he failed to mention the secret evening lessons he'd been receiving for the last several months? These were not from actor and friend, Kadrun Black but from Kad's girlfriend, Cleo.

"You make teleporting seem easy, Cleo," he had told her after his first successful translocation. "You should be teaching the class."

~ ~ ~

And as if Jeori Kellogg had waved a magic wand and decreed it done, at the age of eighteen, Cleopatra

Murphy *did* end up teaching Teleportation I, taking over for the retiring Mz. Landon through an odd series of events that left her in charge.

~ ~ ~

A strange thing had happened after Kad's talk to Art Pod about his experiences in the tunnel and after the video was shown to the rest of the quad and finally sent around the world. With all the new understandings and preparation and waiting for the aliens' next move, what had happened was *absolutely nothing*—no more bad dreams, no black holes, and no feelings of being watched by anyone, anywhere on the planet.

Kadrun had his own theory about that. He remembered the last time he had felt someone watching. It was that day of excitement and first kisses with Cleo. *My elf,* he thought. The aliens must have heard the plans for their defeat and given up on Earth then and there. Could it really be that easy? Kad thought that it could.

~ Epilogue ~

Kad glanced out the small bedroom window, his eyes landing on the yellow roses growing by the corner of the walkway. His thoughts drifted back through the years to all that had happened in the months following the distribution of that video seen 'round the world.

Just a week after the vid was released, he had heard through Cleo that an old art student named John Willets had passed away in his sleep. Recalling the ex-prisoner's story told on that cold November day the year before, Kad wrote a first person monologue in the old man's honor. And he decided to play the part of John Willets himself.

Kad presented his one man work in Professor Potate's class, "The Art of Storytelling." The aging professor was so impressed, not just with the story but with Kadrun's use of accent and body language, that he suggested Kad repeat the one man work on the main stage before the entire quad. And it was a surprise hit!

Meanwhile thanks and congratulations were coming in from around the globe for Kad's vid account of his meet and defeat of the dark forces. It was one day a few months later that Jerry "Jingo" Turner, a former Actors' Pod student and one of the best known producers of old style movies anywhere, paid a surprise call on his old professor, Magnum Potate. He offered to provide enough credits for young actor Kadrun Black and a friend of his choice to make a five day trip to New Hollywood, the movie making capitol of the world—a near replica of the original Hollywood, now a popular scuba diving location. Turner wished to discuss with Kad the possibility of creating a movie about the teenager's frightening adventure.

Kadrun had laughed when he first heard this. Hadn't his friend Jeori suggested the very same thing? So of course it was Jeori Kellogg that Kad chose to accompany him. During their time with the Western Movie Guild, the two received an introduction to movie production and watched the filming of several movies. Then there was a meeting with the man himself, Jerry "Jingo" Turner.

Kad and Jeori were also treated to a day at the Movieland Memorial Theme Park where they saw re-creations of old movie sets from the before time as well as some from the modern age. There was a mock-up of a dusty frontier town from an old Wild West movie topped off with a showdown recreated by two robot "gunslingers." They saw the set of the 2061 movie, "Spacerunner5," with a silver-suited robot playing the part of Captain Mark Claiborne.

To Jeori's delight they also visited the set of "Green Garden Gnomes," a movie Jeori fondly remembered from his early childhood. As they stood watching the small Gnome-bots run around the garden pulling up carrots and beets to frustrate the human gardeners, a particularly tiny gnome ran right off the set and straight up Jeori's pant leg!

But Jeori Kellogg knew just what to do. He grabbed the little guy in the same way as eight-year-old Charlie had in the movie and said "Bad gnome!" in the very same voice. Kad had laughed like crazy at that.

Since then months had passed—and then years. But Kad never heard one word back from New Hollywood about making that movie. Still the idea was not dead. Kad's determined friend Jeori simply wouldn't let it die. And that was that.

2065

~ ~ ~

Twenty five-year-old Kadrun Black shifted his gaze from the window as he pushed back his shoulder-length hair. *And now my life has become something I could never have imagined was possible ten years ago. So many changes....*

Kad ran his hand over the top of the crib that Jeori's friend Mr. Grant had presented to the Quad shortly before his transition to spirit. Jeori had shared with Kad that he had actually spotted his old neighbor on Earth Two one day while he was traveling out in Advanced Interdimensional Travel class. Kadrun shivered. After what he had experienced in that tunnel, he still felt no desire to dem pop ever again.

The young man looked down inside the crib and smiled. Little Eve had somehow kicked a leg out of her covers again. *What a wiggly little angel you are.* He carefully lifted the edge of the soft pink blanket and gently tucked it once more around his daughter's sleeping form.

At nine months of age, little Evie was the great joy of her parents' lives. The only part of her looks she shared with her father was her thick mop of black hair. The rest—her green eyes, small perfect nose and rose petal lips—were all Cleo. Even the way she kicked off her covers in her sleep was just like her mother. For all these reasons Kad had taken to calling her "Little Elf."

Cleo popped her head in the door. "At it again are you, Papa?" she asked softly. Cleo walked over and squeezed Kadrun's hand.

He nodded. "I just can't seem to get enough of watching her sleep."

"I know what you mean. She's so beautiful.

"Love, I came in to tell you that Jeori just called. He's on his way over. He sounded really excited, but he wouldn't say why. Maybe he got something new for the screenplay you two are working on." She tilted her head. "Oh! That was fast. I do believe Jeori just teleported into our living room."

"Yeah, I felt it, too. You taught him too well, Elf."

"I think you may be right. But he was my first student, and I was as excited as he was."

~ ~ ~

A tall, slim twenty-one-year-old Jeori Kellogg poked his head into the nursery and motioned to Kad who joined him in the living room of the small home.

"Everything all right, Jeori?"

"Sure! And Kayla says 'Hi.' She is really starting to show since the last time we visited you and Cleo. Oh, and I haven't told you that we discovered that there's a family home coming vacant close to you. It's right down the street and.... Guess what? We got it reserved! We'll be neighbors, Kad. Our kids can go to the same playhouse and everything!"

"That's such good news, Jeori. Cleo will be pleased, too."

Jeori nodded. "Sometimes we can hardly wait for the twins to be born. Neither of us can believe we still have two more months to wait—especially Kayla. She's afraid she'll be as big as a barn by then."

"Two babies will really keep you jumping. Get your sleep now while you can. That's my best advice. So Jeori...is that what you were so in a hurry to tell me about?"

"That's only part of it. I finally know what the last part of the story should be! And I also know how we can set the scene! I've been working on the title, too, but that's giving me more trouble." He scratched his head.

Kad's eyes crinkled at his friend's obvious excitement, and he tried to hide a smile. No matter how old Jeori got, he would never entirely grow up. And as far as Kad was concerned, that was a good thing. Jeori's enthusiasm and stubbornness in keeping his dreams alive had created magical outcomes more than once...and not just for himself but for everyone around him.

Kadrun took a deep breath. "I've been playing with ideas for the title, too. So what did you come up with?"

"At first I thought it should be "The Hungry Dark Prepares to Feed on Kadrun Black," but that's w-a-a-ay too long, isn't it?"

Kad chuckled. Then he laughed out loud. He couldn't help himself. It was the silliest title he had ever heard.

"Well, I did say it needed work."

Kad rubbed a tear of laughter from the corner of his eye and took another breath. "Yes...yes, you did say that. So...you said you got the final scene?"

"Yeah. Okay. So remember that set with the inside of a spaceship we saw all those years ago at the Movieland Theme Park?"

"Sure. What about it?"

"Well, suppose that we have the aliens on a spaceship somewhere say...near the edge of the Milky Way. There is a scene with this gigantic ship floating in space. Then the scene cuts to inside the ship. And just suppose the aliens look down through this portal that connects them to Earth where they see you kissing Cleo under that tree.

They feel all wrecked because they've heard about the vid you're going to make, and they realize that they will be *totally* defeated if they stay around. *So* the grand Leader tells them they will leave and go pick on another planet and convince those people to be scared and angry and guilty and all the rest so they can control them next. Grand Leader makes up some excuse like this is a crummy planet anyway...see? And then there's chanting and...and...."

A small smile came to Kadrun's face, and he held up his hand. "And then Grand Leader says," Kad continued, 'This peace and love nonsense cannot last forever. We will return in two hundred years. By then they will have forgotten all about us and we will ....'

"....try again...try again...try again," finished the two friends in unison.

"It really happened!" Jeori exclaimed in wonder.

"That's my guess."

~ ~ ~

Loud squalling erupted in the nursery. Little Eve was awake...and from the sound of her cries, she was *hungry.* Her father jumped up and moved quickly down the hall towards the nursery door. "Dibs on feeding her!" he called to his mate.

"Later, Kad ...."

Kadrun turned back to say goodbye to his friend.

But Jeori Kellogg had already disappeared.

2065
In the Beginning

...depicts a probable future containing a simple and creative way for human beings to live on and with the Earth.

Now what can *you* imagine?

Dream the World
Live the Dream!

Krista Markowitz is founder and CEO of Her Own Life. She loves digging in the earth, laughing with family and friends, free-style oil painting, and channeling surprising stories. Krista has also authored *Mrs. Tipperwillow's Afterlife Adventures*, a book about the spirit world for kids and kids at heart, and *About Afterlife: Two Kid's Stories* which is available through her website.

www.tipperwillow.com